PERFECT PASSER

- As the football coach in Kiln, Mississippi, Brett Favre's father taught his son the lessons that have made Brett a superior leader on the field; those lessons include the belief that the team should come before personal glory.

- During a successful college career, Brett amazed everyone by returning from a horrible car accident to break many of the quarterback records at the University of Southern Mississippi.

- At the age of twenty-eight, Brett Favre has already won the Super Bowl and two National Football Conference titles for the Green Bay Packers, earning comparisons to the legendary quarterbacks of the past.

Here's Brett Favre, from his years as a two-sport high school athlete in Mississippi to his record-breaking three Most Valuable Player National Football League titles. Read all about the quarterback who's truly in a league of his own.

BRETT FAVRE:
A Biography

Books by Bill Gutman

Sports Illustrated: Baseball's Record Breakers
Sports Illustrated: Great Moments in Baseball
Sports Illustrated: Great Moments in Pro Football
Sports Illustrated: Pro Football's Record Breakers
Baseball Super Teams
Bo Jackson: A Biography
Brett Favre: A Biography
Football Super Teams
Grant Hill: A Biography
Great Quarterbacks of the NFL
Great Sports Upsets
Great Sports Upsets 2
Ken Griffey, Jr.: A Biography
Michael Jordan: A Biography
NBA High-Flyers
Pro Sports Champions
Shaquille O'Neal: A Biography
Tiger Woods: A Biography

Available from ARCHWAY Paperbacks

BRETT FAVRE

A Biography

BILL GUTMAN

AN ARCHWAY PAPERBACK
Published by POCKET BOOKS
New York London Toronto Sydney Tokyo Singapore

AN ARCHWAY PAPERBACK *Original*

An Archway Paperback published by
POCKET BOOKS, a division of Simon & Schuster Inc.
1230 Avenue of the Americas, New York, NY 10020

Copyright © 1998 by Bill Gutman

ISBN: 0-671-02077-3

First Archway Paperback printing September 1998

10 9 8 7 6 5 4 3 2 1

AN ARCHWAY PAPERBACK and colophon are
registered trademarks of Simon & Schuster Inc.

Front cover photo credits: large photo by Jonathan Daniel/Allsport,
inset photo by Scott Halleran/Allsport

Printed in the U.S.A.

IL 7+

To a good friend,
Shawn Frederick

BRETT FAVRE

A Biography

Introduction

Most franchise quarterbacks in the National Football League come well prepared for the job. They cut their teeth in Pop Warner or on the sandlots, then excel as stars in high school. From there, the major colleges fight for the young athletes in unabashed recruiting wars. Once the coaches make their choices, the players begin chucking the football at the college level, honing their skills, working with top receivers and usually a pro-type formation. It's all the perfect training ground.

Then the best of the best—quarterbacks like John Elway, Dan Marino, and Drew Bledsoe—become first-round draft choices and, with high expectations, go about making their mark as pros. Some college stars need more time to adjust to the pro game than others. They serve as backups for a year or two before taking over. Others are thrown into action as rookies and must sink or swim on their own.

But by and large, the majority of great NFL quarterbacks come into the league with their reputations preceding them. Occasionally a sleeper—a quarterback who arrives out of nowhere—will emerge to become a superstar. Perhaps the most famous of the rags-to-riches quarterbacks was the legendary Johnny Unitas. A ninth-round pick out of the University of Louisville in the mid-1950s, Unitas was promptly cut by the Pittsburgh Steelers. The next year, when he was playing semipro ball, the Baltimore Colts called and asked if he was still looking for work.

Unitas went on to become the greatest passer of his generation, a record breaker who still holds the NFL mark of throwing a touchdown pass in forty-seven straight games. In fact, there are some who still call Johnny U. the best ever. But with so many college programs emphasizing the passing game, and with the sophisticated scouting combines, it would be difficult for a top quarterback to be passed over in the football world of the 1990s.

That's what makes the case of Brett Favre so unusual. Today the quarterback of the 1996 Super Bowl champion Green Bay Packers is being called the best in the game. He is known for his toughness and rocket arm, for his ability to create big plays, and for the competitive fire that fuels his tremendous will to win. Yet his climb to the top is one of the great success stories of recent years.

BRETT FAVRE: A Biography

The quarterback who excels on the frozen turf at Lambeau Field in Green Bay actually grew up in a tiny town on a Mississippi bayou. So isolated was he there that not one major college recruited him. So there would be no glamorous college career and no appearances on national television to bolster him.

Brett attended the only Division I school that showed any interest in him—the University of Southern Mississippi. There he began to emerge from anonymity. He showed himself to be a fearless, strong-armed quarterback capable of producing big numbers. He loved it when his team upset nationally ranked schools, but that didn't mean NFL scouts saw him as a can't-miss prospect.

He was taken in the second round of the 1991 draft by the Atlanta Falcons. As a rookie he was nothing more than a third-string quarterback who was active for only three of his team's sixteen games. He also ended the season in the doghouse for his allegedly lackadaisical attitude, and he was called uncoachable. This was not a master plan for future stardom.

Fortunately for Brett, the Packers, and the NFL, an off-season trade to Green Bay provided him with a second chance. Before the 1992 season ended, Brett found himself the starting quarterback when an injury shelved the Packers' top guy. The sudden leap from third string to starter would have overwhelmed some players, but Brett made the most of his opportunity. He's been at the helm of the Green Bay offense ever since.

Not that there haven't been some setbacks. A

serious car accident almost cost him his senior year at college. He then had to survive his frustrating rookie season in Atlanta. In Green Bay there were times when the strong-willed Favre and his strong-willed coach, Mike Holmgren, clashed over the running of the offense. Later, when he was established as a star, Brett refused to come out of the lineup despite a succession of painful injuries, which led to an unwitting addiction to painkillers.

He faced that crisis the same way he always faced adversity—head on. Again he turned a negative into a positive, and he emerged as one of the best quarterbacks of his generation. Brett is the first quarterback ever to throw for thirty or more touchdowns in four straight seasons. He is also the first NFL player to be named the league's Most Valuable Player three years running. With a great team behind him, Brett Favre has had the opportunity to perform on the biggest football stage of all—the Super Bowl—two seasons in a row.

Call it an unlikely story, but fortunately for football fans everywhere, it's true. And it's far from over. At the beginning of the 1998 season, Brett Favre will be only twenty-eight years old. The kid from the South who made his name in the North, and who is now known everywhere, still has a lot of football years left.

for those who have grown up around it, the bayou is just another part of life.

Most of the 7,500 or so longtime residents of Kiln (pronounced Kill) are used to places with names like Beat and Bang Auto Body and the Twist and Shout Bait Shop. They are places the Favre family knows well, too.

Irvin Favre Road is named for Brett's father. He earned the honor partly because he's had a nearly thirty-year career as a high school baseball and football coach at Hancock North Central High School in Kiln. The other reason may be that the Favres and their relatives were the only families living on the road.

Brett was actually born in Gulfport, Mississippi, on October 10, 1969. He was the second of Irvin and Bonita Favre's four children. Scott was the oldest, then came Brett, then younger brother Jeff, and finally sister Brandi. Before long the family of six had moved to Kiln, near the Rotten Bayou.

Mr. and Mrs. Favre settled in to teach and coach at Hancock North Central. Bonita Favre taught special education while her husband handled the coaching. And they set about raising their family of four very active kids. The boys were usually into something. If they weren't fishing for crawfish, they were climbing trees and shooting BB guns. And of course they began playing sports early.

Like most kids, they were into a little of everything: baseball, football, basketball. Brett always had a strong arm, which most people figured he'd inherited from his father, who had been a pitcher at Southern Mississippi. But years later Brett gave another version, crediting his mother, who had played a great deal of softball in her youth.

"I always thought I got my arm from my father," he said, "until one summer just a few years ago. My mother got mad at me, threw a pastrami sandwich, and hit me in the head. Hard. She really had something on that sandwich."

Obviously, Brett got his athletic ability from both parents. Although young Brett liked all sports, two of his earliest idols were football quarterbacks who played in the South. One was Archie Manning, a star at the University of Mississippi and later with the New Orleans Saints. The other was Roger Staubach, who became one of the greats with the Dallas Cowboys. In fact, Brett wrote in a school essay in the sixth grade at Bay Saint Louis Elementary School that he wanted to be a professional football player when he grew up.

But as a youngster he played every sport. In fact, all four Favre kids played youth sports. Their parents tried to follow all of them, racing from field to field during times when the kids were in different leagues at the same time.

"There were a couple of times when I ended up on the wrong field," Irvin Favre said.

When Brett wasn't playing sports or having fun with his brothers and friends, he was in school. It wasn't the way most kids are in school. Brett Favre was *really* in school. From the time he was in the third grade until he graduated from high school, he never missed a day. Not one single day! His perfect-attendance streak lasted some ten years and was an early indication of Brett's toughness and sense of responsibility. His parents always stressed responsibility and the importance of not disappointing the people who were counting on him.

"My parents were teachers," Brett explained, "so it was tough to play hooky. Even if I was sick, I would tough it out and go to class."

That attainment in itself may be one of Brett's greatest records. But there were a lot more achievements to come, especially on the athletic field. When he was in the eighth grade, Brett was already a good enough baseball player to become the starting third baseman for the Hancock North Central High School team. He led the team in hitting that year with a .325 average. In fact, he would be the leading hitter for five straight seasons.

Brett's high school baseball career came off without a hitch, but it wasn't the same with football. While he was good enough to play baseball as an eighth grader, he wasn't quite big enough to play football. Also, there were players ahead of him. When he finally had a chance to take over the quarterback spot during his sophomore year, he was sidelined with mononucleosis and missed the entire season.

So Brett entered his junior year in 1985 having never quarterbacked a high school football team. Thus his talents were unknown. He was now 6 feet 2 and weighed a solid 185 pounds, and he could throw the heck out of a football. The game, however, is littered with big kids who can throw but just don't have a feel for running an offense or the instincts to make it all work. There was some other news that year that would have disappointed any kid who liked to throw the football.

The Hancock Hawks had a mediocre 4–6 record in 1984, and Coach Favre decided to make a change for the upcoming season. He was going to have the team run the wishbone offense, a formation the Hawks had used to great success in the 1970s. Because he had a number of outstanding runners, the coach felt the Hawks could move the ball on the ground against anyone. The wishbone was essentially a running formation.

In the wishbone, the quarterback usually takes the snap and immediately rolls out to the left or right. He then pitches the ball to a trailing back or, sometimes, runs with it himself. Rarely does he have the opportunity to throw. That's the way Coach Favre wanted it. He had a big offensive line that could block, a number of solid runners, and one really outstanding ball carrier in Charles Burton.

So the team ran out of the wishbone in 1985. Sure enough, they began winning, and Charles Burton was on his way to a big season on the ground. Brett did his job competently, but because he didn't throw much, he wasn't regarded as anything more than a tough high school quarterback, a good soldier.

The Hancock Hawks were a 6–4 team that year, with Charles Burton the featured back running for more than 1,000 yards. Brett got to throw the football just 97 times in 10 games. He completed 40 passes for 723 yards and 8 touchdowns. Considering that Hancock ran out of the wishbone, those weren't bad numbers. But they weren't the kind that would put Brett on a short list of quarterback prospects for the major colleges.

It didn't look to get any better the next year. Brett was a senior in 1986, and for that season his father decided to use the Wing-T and Power-I formations, both designed for running. Charles Burton was returning, and the Hawks expected to ride to victory on his quick legs. Despite the fact that he wouldn't be throwing a lot, Brett worked hard to become familiar with the new formations. He wouldn't leave the field until he got each play right and the coaches were satisfied. In other words, he planned to make the most of his situation and do whatever he could to help his team win.

So at the outset of Brett's senior year, college recruiters didn't flock to Kiln to see this strong-armed quarterback. The reason was simple—he didn't have much of a chance to show off the strong arm. No one really knew about it. The only Division I school that had a clue about Brett was his father's alma mater, the University of Southern Mississippi.

The recruiter who covered Hancock County for Southern Miss was its offensive line coach, Mark McHale. It was his first year at the school, and the list of prospects he was given did not include Brett Favre. McHale's job was to check those already on the list, screening the players to see which ones looked like true prospects and which weren't living up to their advance billing. As McHale traveled to the various high schools in Hancock County, more than one coach asked him if he had seen the quarterback for Hancock North Central. Of course he hadn't.

The descriptions he was hearing made Brett sound like a pretty good athlete who didn't have real speed and didn't throw much. Kids like that rarely become Division I quarterbacks. But when several rival coaches suggested checking Brett out, McHale decided to have a look. It didn't hurt that Irvin Favre was a Southern Miss alumnus. Irvin told McHale flat out that he thought his son could play college ball. He gave him a tape of Brett in action, but it didn't show McHale much.

"The tape was almost all running plays," McHale said. "The three or four throws Brett made were play-action passes that any kid could have completed."

There was no way McHale could make a commitment to a high school quarterback based on a tape that mainly showed him handing the ball off to his running backs. But he decided to return and watch Brett one more time. Even with a college recruiter in the stands, Irvin Favre didn't alter his game plan to showcase his son. Brett threw only three passes. That might have ended it, except for one thing: Mark McHale had watched Brett warm up.

"I could see he had lots of pop on the ball," he said. "It was obvious he had a great arm. I decided to come back and see him once more."

Brett was already showing the kind of confidence he would take to the pros. When he met

Mark McHale for the first time, he said quickly, "Coach, I can play for you. I know I can."

But he still had to show the man what he could do on the field. Coach Favre had told McHale that he would open up the offense the next time and let Brett throw more. But when the Southern Miss coach showed up, the Hawks ran the same game plan as before. Coach Favre just couldn't change, even for the sake of his son. He wanted to win the game and felt he could do that best by having his team run the football. Instead of throwing three times, Brett threw four passes. But that fourth and final pass may have changed the course of Brett's career and altered the history of the Green Bay Packers.

Mark McHale remembers the first three passes being short ones that anyone could have thrown. But the fourth—that was one he says he'll never forget.

"[Brett] rolled out to the right hash mark and just zoomed the ball sixty yards to the end zone. . . . The football had smoke and fire coming out of it. I decided then and there that Brett was a big, big-time possibility. . . . God only gives out so many arms like that."

After that the Southern Miss people began watching Brett very closely. It didn't hurt that the Hancock Hawks were having a successful season. Charles Burton was still the main weapon in the attack, with Brett throwing only when absolutely necessary. The team won its first seven games and was ranked number nine in the state. It was that seventh win in which Brett showed what he was made of.

Hancock was playing Long Beach High, and Brett was having a great game. He scored his team's first touchdown on a 25-yard run. Then he threw a 6-yard touchdown pass and also threw for a 2-point conversion, making the score 14–0. Long Beach then battled back to make it 14–7. Then a 47-yard TD scamper by Charles Burton and another 2-point conversion pass by Brett made it 22–7. Shortly afterward, Burton was ejected from the game for a personal foul. With the best runner gone, Brett had to take over.

Long Beach didn't quit, either. They rallied to tie the game at 22–22. Finally the Hawks got the ball at their own 41-yard line with just 59 seconds left. At this point Brett was playing in pain.

"I had cramps in both legs," he said. "I couldn't move. I think . . . everybody was expecting that we'd wind up tied."

Brett managed to return to the field and lead a last-minute drive. He completed passes of 16 and 12 yards. A couple of running plays put the Hawks on the Long Beach 4-yard line. Despite the cramps, Brett carried the ball on an option and got it to the one. There was time for just one more play.

Brett looked to the sidelines. His father was signaling for a handoff, with the running back diving off-tackle. But when Brett brought his team to the line of scrimmage, he looked at the defense and decided a quarterback sneak had a better chance of working. He called signals to change the play, then took the ball into the end zone for the winning score.

As the team celebrated on the field with their fans flocking out to greet them, Irvin Favre made a beeline for his son and began berating him for changing the play.

"I wanted him to know he had to respect the coach's decision," Mr. Favre said. "We had a certain way of doing things, and I didn't want a young kid going against my calls. It didn't matter that he was my own boy—except maybe I was madder."

Coach Favre knew it was a great victory for his team, but he felt he had to maintain a line of discipline between coach and player. Later he would admit that "Brett played just a super football game—maybe the best he's ever played. He ran hard, threw, and played defense. He's a real competitor."

He also knew his son had a strong will, which was a characteristic of all the Favres. Brett's willingness to take risks and do things his own way has led to his making mistakes over the years. But this impulsiveness is also part of the total package that would make Brett a great leader and great quarterback. His quarterback sneak, against orders, kept his team unbeaten to that point.

Two late-season losses put something of a damper on the season, however. The Hawks finished at 8–2, losing to a powerful D'Iberville team, 28–6, for the District VIII, Class 4-A title. Brett's numbers weren't much different from those of the year before, although his teammates knew what a great player he had become. In fact, his receivers often said he threw so hard that it was difficult for them to catch the ball. Hearing that, his father had to remind Brett to let up just a little on his passes.

So the great arm was there, but no one outside of Mississippi knew about it. Only Mark McHale from Southern Mississippi had any idea of Brett's potential. But did he and the other coaches at Southern Miss rate Brett high enough to offer him a scholarship?

Though Brett still wasn't sure what the future held, he did have an unusual experience in the spring of his senior year. He made his first long trip out of the Deep South, when his senior class traveled to New York and Boston. They had raised the money for the trip themselves with a number of special projects. In Boston, Brett learned first-hand about the culinary differences in various parts of the country. It is something he still laughs about today.

"I went to a restaurant, a sandwich place, in Boston," Brett recalled. "The guy said, 'What'll you have?' I told him I guessed I'd have a shrimp po'boy. He just looked at me. I tried to explain what a shrimp po'boy was. I wound up with a submarine sandwich."

Brett was happy to return to the familiar sights and sounds of Hancock County and Kiln. Little did he know then that he would someday make his mark far from home in the sometimes frigid North.

Chapter 2

Joining the Golden Eagles

Mark McHale admitted that while Southern Mississippi had an interest in Brett, he was at the bottom of their prospect list. But the more they saw of him and learned about him, the higher his stock rose. Yet he wasn't a shoo-in. When the scholarships were being handed out for 1987, Brett still hadn't been chosen. He knew the odds were against him.

"I was never recruited for college," he said. "No one really wanted me. Coming from Kiln, playing for a small school, and not really putting up big numbers . . . well, nobody knows who you are."

Finally it came down to the last scholarship. Mark McHale kept pushing for Brett. He raved about Brett's throwing arm, but none of the other coaches had seen him throw. McHale said Brett would make a fine free safety on defense if he didn't make it as a quarterback. He didn't really believe that, but he wanted Brett to have that scholarship.

Finally the other coaches agreed. Brett Favre was offered a scholarship to study and play football at the University of Southern Mississippi. The final decision had literally come down to the wire.

"Three days before the signing date, I was going to either Pearl River Junior College or Delta State," Brett explained.

Yet Mark McHale suspected that Brett was finally chosen partly because Irvin Favre was an alumnus and the athletic department wanted to keep the lines open to other athletes in Hancock County and that entire part of the state. The coaches still weren't sure Brett would emerge as a top-flight quarterback. But Brett felt proud that he would at least have a chance.

"If anyone ever defied the odds, it was me," Brett said. "I knew a place like Hancock County rarely put out big-time athletes. But I never gave up. Southern Miss really took me as a defensive back. When I went there as a freshman, I worked out both ways at first. And I was the seventh quarterback on the depth chart. But I kept believing, because the one thing you don't ever want to do is look back and say, 'I wish.' "

So in the late summer of 1987, Brett traveled to Hattiesburg, Mississippi, to enroll at Southern Miss and begin football practice. He was still 6 feet 2, but he now weighed more than 200 pounds. He was bucking the odds, though. When he looked at the depth chart, he saw six quarterbacks listed ahead of him. Many on the coaching staff still regarded him as a defensive back, but that didn't bother Brett.

"I've always had to struggle for what I've got," Brett said later. "I was always the underdog."

Only this time the underdog didn't take long to show everyone he wasn't a defensive back. When he began throwing the football around on the very first day of practice, heads turned.

"Coaches stopped what they were doing and just looked over from wherever they were," said long-time assistant coach Thamus Coleman. "Brett walked out there from the first day, and it was like he'd been doing this all his life. He could see every inch of the field, he knew every route, he just zinged the ball to receivers. It was unbelievable."

Brett continued to impress, even after the upperclassmen had joined the freshmen at practice. It wasn't long before he was moved up to number three on the depth chart. He was still just seventeen years old and from a small high school where he hadn't thrown much. Yet he wasn't even nervous when he quarterbacked a scrimmage against the first-unit defense. He fired the ball all over the field, and the defense was hard-pressed to contain him. Now even head coach Jim Carmody was impressed.

"You know what?" Carmody said. "If a kid impresses my own defense that darn much, maybe I've got to get him in there."

But as the number three QB, Brett wasn't getting many snaps in practice. He would practice with the scout team, players who weren't expected to get in the games. Despite this, he had surprising confidence and even declared to Mark McHale that he was ready to play.

Southern Mississippi was far from a national football power. But because they were a Division I school in the Deep South, they were scheduled to play such traditional powerhouses as Alabama, Auburn, Florida State, the University of Mississippi, and Texas A&M. This didn't make it easy for Southern Miss, but there were times when the Golden Eagles were able to pull off an upset. Brett learned that those were the moments the players lived for.

"Southern Miss was a place where everyone had been rejected by the big schools for some reason," he said. "We were the Island of Misfits. We thrived on that. We'd play Alabama, Auburn, and there would be stories in the papers about how we'd been rejected by them. We'd come out and win the game, and guys would be yelling on the field, 'What's wrong with us now?' It was a great way to play."

The first game of the 1987 season was against Alabama at Birmingham. Brett, being third string, didn't get in the game, and the Crimson Tide rolled over the Golden Eagles, 38–6.

As Mark McHale would later say, the Southern Miss offense looked as if it didn't exist. "We not only didn't move the ball," he said. "It looked as if we would never move it."

Tulane was coming to Hattiesburg the following week for the Southern Miss home opener. Coach Carmody kept hearing from the media and alumni all week about how dreadful the Golden Eagles offense looked. Finally he decided to take a look at the freshman, Favre, maybe as soon as the upcoming Tulane game. But Brett was still working with the third string and had little real preparation. If a freshman is thrown to the wolves with no preparation and is overwhelmed, the experience can sometimes completely destroy his confidence. But even without work with the first unit, Brett kept telling people he was ready.

Ailrick Young, a junior, was the starting QB for the Golden Eagles against Tulane, as some 16,000 fans at Roberts Stadium wondered if the freshman with the rocket arm would see action. Tulane wasn't a powerhouse in 1987, either, and the game was nearly an offensive stalemate. At the half, Southern Miss had a 7–3 lead, but the team hadn't really been moving the ball.

Then, early in the third quarter, Tulane scored and went ahead, 10–7. By this time second-string QB Simmie Carter was in the game. Southern Miss intercepted a Tulane pass in their own territory, but Carter could move the club only 16 yards before the drive stalled. Fortunately the Golden Eagles were close enough for a tying field goal, making it a 10–10 game. Tulane then moved in for another score. They missed the extra point, but it was a 16–10 game now, and the way the Southern Miss offense was looking, it just might stay that way.

Young then returned to the game but couldn't move the offense on the next series. That was when Coach Carmody turned to Brett and said, "Warm up."

Brett was immediately pumped. He began jumping up and down on the sidelines, getting himself loose and ready to rip. Even the other players were surprised by the coach's decision. Many thought the plan would be to redshirt him, which meant keeping him out of games so that he would have four full years of eligibility following his freshman year. But now he was going to enter the second game of the season.

With 9:35 left in the third period, Brett trotted onto the gridiron and joined his team in the huddle. That was when he finally realized what was happening.

"I was scared," he admitted later. "It was quite an experience running out there. When I went in, I just didn't know where to throw the ball. My mind felt like it was blown. So I just kept the ball and ran."

Many football players need a good hit to settle them down, and Brett ran a keeper for no gain. But being tackled by several Tulane defenders helped rid him of the jitters. His first completion was just a 7-yarder, and the team had to punt. But the next time he came out, he began playing aggressive, self-assured football.

He led the Golden Eagles on a solid drive and capped it with a 7-yard touchdown pass to Chris McGee. He had to roll to his right to avoid a Tulane blitz, and he threw on the run for the score. The extra point gave Southern Miss a 17–16 lead.

Before the game ended, Brett led the Golden Eagles on two more scoring drives, capping the second with a 23-yard touchdown strike to Alfred Williams that provided the margin in a 31–24 victory.

Teammate Jim Ferrell was one of many who attributed the victory to the play of the freshman quarterback from Kiln. "Brett came in and was the spark," Ferrell said. "In his second series we knew all we had to do was hold them out and we were going down the field."

Brett's great debut didn't mean the rest of the season would all be smooth sailing. On October 10, his eighteenth birthday, Brett started against powerful Florida State. He would learn a lesson in humility as the Seminoles humbled the Golden Eagles, 61–10, while the Florida State fans sang a sarcastic "Happy Birthday" to Brett. But all the great ones know how to bounce back. It wasn't long before Brett convinced everyone he was for real.

Against Southwestern Louisiana he completed 21 of 39 passes for a school record 295 yards. The downside was that the defense wasn't up to the task and Southern Miss lost, 37–30. But in victories over East Carolina and Louisville, Brett lit up the board, firing for three scores in each game. He also engineered an 18–14 victory over a tough rival, Mississippi State.

With Brett at the helm, the Golden Eagles offense averaged nearly 27 points a game. He was still learning, still raw in many ways. But he had already demonstrated his ability to put points on the board with a suddenness and an explosiveness that would always worry opposing defenses. A defense could never relax with Brett Favre on the field.

The 1987 season ended with the Golden Eagles compiling a 6–5 record. Brett completed 79 of 194 passes for 1,264 yards and a school record 14 touchdowns. His inexperience showed in his completing just 40.7 percent of his passes. He also threw 13 interceptions. But overall he had established himself, given his team an explosive offense, and shown everyone a glimpse of a future that suddenly looked very bright.

Chapter 3

A Near Tragedy

Southern Mississippi made some coaching changes prior to the 1988 season. Curley Hallman took over as head coach, and former Golden Eagles quarterback, Jeff Bower, returned as offensive coordinator. It didn't take Coach Bower long to recognize the asset the team had in Brett Favre. Seeing Brett's arm strength and overall talent, he quickly changed the offense to make the most of his sophomore quarterback's talent. And as soon as he began working with Brett, Jeff Bower became a fan.

"Brett was just a great kid who wanted to get better," Bower said. "He was as intelligent a player as I've ever been around. Football just made sense to him. He understood things right away, which most guys don't."

Coach Bower set out to refine Brett's game. He

wanted to convert him from a thrower to a passer. As the coach explained, throwers with strong arms like Brett's feel they can cut loose at any time and throw into tight coverage. "Forcing the ball into cracks" was the way Bower put it. The new offense gave Brett more options and opened up the field. Hopefully, he wouldn't have to force the ball so much, and his completion percentage would rise.

With the new offense, with other fine players returning, and with Brett Favre a year better, Southern Miss began to play outstanding football. Before long, Brett Favre was looking like a human highlight film all by himself. In a wild game against East Carolina, the Golden Eagles trailed, 42–38. With time running down, they were 74 yards away from the winning touchdown. Brett was having a great day despite painful leg cramps that had begun in the first half.

Nevertheless he began marching his team upfield. With the clock continuing to run, Brett had his club at the East Carolina 47-yard line. Once again he dropped back to pass. He was chased from the pocket but managed to unload a long pass downfield. Wide receiver Alfred Williams grabbed the ball just as he was tackled at the 5-yard line. Back upfield, Brett lay motionless on the turf. The cramps had struck again, and he absolutely couldn't continue. His backup, Ailrick Young, came on and threw a short TD pass to give the Golden Eagles a 45–42 victory.

But it was Brett's performance that had everyone talking. He had completed 20 of 32 passes for 301 yards, the first 300-plus passing day in school history. Receiver Williams, who caught the key 42-yarder, seemed to reach up for the ball at the last second without looking. Asked later how he knew the ball was coming, Williams answered, "I heard it whistling."

Whether that story was entirely true or not, it showed the force with which Brett could throw the ball. Many of his passes did indeed whistle through the air to his receivers.

That wasn't Brett's only big game that year, either. Against Louisville he completed another 20 of 32 for 275 yards, and against Memphis State he connected on 19 of 36 for 241 yards. He also threw for three touchdowns in games against Virginia Tech, Tulane, and Southwestern Louisiana. Against SW Louisiana, he completed 23 of 30 passes, a 76.7 success percentage.

When Southern Miss met national power Auburn, Brett had a career best 25 completions in 43 attempts, but the Golden Eagles were beaten, 38–8. The only other game the team lost was to another powerhouse, 29–13 to Florida State. But they had big wins as well. Besides the great comeback against East Carolina, Southern Miss topped Virginia Tech, 35–13, and Mississippi State, 38–21. The Golden Eagles finished the regular season at 9–2 and were invited to play in the Independence Bowl against the University of Texas at El Paso.

Brett used that occasion to cap off a great year. He connected on 15 of 26 passes for 157 yards and a touchdown as the Golden Eagles won it easily, 38–18. The team completed a 10–2 slate, and

Brett produced a season in which he set a number of school records.

Overall, he completed 178 of 319 passes for 2,271 yards. His passing percentage was up to 55.8, a big improvement over the 40.7 of his freshman year. He broke his own school record by throwing for 16 scores and set another Southern Miss mark by throwing at least one touchdown pass in each of nine consecutive games. That wasn't all.

His five interceptions in 319 attempts gave him a 1.57 interception ratio. That was the lowest among the nation's top fifty passers. And he finished the season with a streak of 144 straight passes without an intercept. To say that Brett Favre had arrived was something of an understatement. In fact he was beginning to attract national attention.

Prior to his junior season of 1989, Brett finally began getting some press notices outside of his native Mississippi. A number of analysts looking at the upcoming season were mentioning his name among the top quarterbacks in the country. Better yet, it looked as if Brett and his entire team were going to get some national publicity.

"A writer came down to Southern Miss to do an article for *Sports Illustrated*," Brett recalled. "He said he wasn't sure the article would be in, but if we beat Florida State in our opener, he was pretty sure it would make it. So we went out and pulled the upset. All I'm thinking about the last few minutes on the field is, 'God, I'm going to be in *Sports Illustrated*.'"

The article never appeared. Apparently it was bumped by something the editors considered more important. But Southern Miss fans who saw the game against Florida State will never forget it. It was one of the great ones. Florida State came into the season ranked number one in the nation. They were led by defensive back Deion Sanders and were 22-point favorites to top the Golden Eagles. In fact during the last two seasons the Seminoles had humbled Southern Miss with scores of 61–10 and 49–13.

This time the game began as if it was going to be more of the same. The Golden Eagles received the opening kickoff. Brett came on and wanted to make a statement. So he dropped back to pass on the very first play of the game. Wouldn't you know it, Deion Sanders used his great quickness to step in front of the receiver and pick the ball off. He then raced into the end zone, dancing the final few steps in true "Prime Time" fashion. One play and Florida State had the lead.

Some quarterbacks would have been defeated right then and there. Not Brett. He began throwing again, and this time he succeeded. By the fourth quarter, Southern Miss had a 24–23 lead, and the scent of upset was in the air. But the Seminoles weren't ranked number one for nothing. In the fourth period they began driving. With just 6:57 remaining, Bill Mason kicked a 27-yard field goal to give Florida State a 26–24 lead. Now it was up to Brett and his teammates to try to get it back.

Once again the game came down to the final drive. With time winding down, Southern Miss was at its own 42-yard line, 58 yards from pay dirt. Brett began driving his team, connecting on short passes mixed with a few running plays. He had to watch the clock as well as the field. It finally came down to this: the Golden Eagles had a third-and-goal at the Florida State 2-yard line; a field goal would win the game. So Coach Hallman signaled a running play. If the back didn't get into the end zone, the ball would be in the middle of the field for a fourth-down try for the field goal.

In the booth above the field, offensive coordinator Jeff Bower disagreed with the coach's call. He felt Florida State would be jamming the middle, opening things up for a rollout pass from Brett for a touchdown.

"Normally I would have agreed with Coach Hallman and gone the conservative way," Bower said. "But Brett gave us the edge. I wouldn't have called a pass with another quarterback, but I felt Brett could pull it off."

Bower told Hallman what he wanted to do, and the team called a time-out. When they told Brett what they were trying to decide, Brett said he'd prefer the rollout pass. The coaches finally agreed. Brett returned to the huddle, called the play, and took the snap. He rolled out to his right as if he intended to run a bootleg play. The Seminole defense came after him. At the last second he lobbed a quick pass to tight end Anthony Harris in the end zone. Touchdown!

Just twenty-three seconds remained in the game when Brett struck. It didn't matter that the extra point was missed. Southern Miss had won, 30–26, thanks to Brett Favre, who threw for 282 yards and two touchdowns against the team that had been ranked the best in the land.

"Before we went to Jacksonville," Brett said, "people would come up to me and tell me if we won the game they would throw us a huge party when we got back to Hattiesburg. But when we won it, we had a pretty great party ourselves on the field. All my life I've dreamed of winning a game like this, especially doing it the way we did."

Brett's great performance didn't go unnoticed. For his efforts he was named Offensive Back of the Week by United Press International. It looked as if Brett and his team were poised on the brink of a great season. But as it turned out, the Southern Miss defense wasn't up to the level of the offense. For that reason, the season wasn't quite what it could have been. But that didn't dim the achievements of Brett Favre.

Following the great upset win over Florida State, the Golden Eagles suddenly went into a tailspin. The team lost to Mississippi State, Auburn, TCU, and Texas A&M in four straight games. Against Texas A&M, Brett completed 21 of 42 passes for 303 yards, then a school record. But the defense couldn't stop the Aggies, and Southern Miss lost, 31–14.

The Golden Eagles stopped the losing streak with a 30–21 victory over Tulane. But their 2–4 mark was already a bitter disappointment, especially after the 10–2 record of a year earlier. With five games left, Brett and his teammates didn't want to quit. On the contrary, they wanted to turn it around and finish strong.

Next came Louisville, a game Southern Miss felt it had to win. It was a struggle. The game was tied at 10–10 in the fourth quarter. Louisville made a last try to score. With thirteen seconds left, Cardinals kicker Ron Bell got set to try a 43-yard field goal to win it. But the Eagles' Vernard Collins partially blocked the kick, and it rolled dead on the Southern Miss 21. Brett and the offense came on with time for perhaps two plays.

On the first play, Brett's receivers were covered and he did well just to get back to the line of scrimmage. Now there was time for one more snap. He dropped back again, scrambled to his right to avoid a charging lineman, then threw the ball as high and as far as he could. It was a typical Hail Mary pass—a wing and a prayer. Several players went for it at once and tipped it in the air. It finally settled into the hands of Eagles receiver Darryl Tillman, who caught it in full stride and ran it into the end zone.

It was a miracle finish. Southern Miss won it, 16–10, with Brett's strong arm once again getting the job done.

"The odds of that happening are unreal," Brett said afterward. "When you go up to the line, you're really thinking the game is going to end in a tie. I'm sure that was everybody's feeling."

A lucky break? Sure. But if Brett hadn't had the arm to get the ball out there, it wouldn't have happened. After that, the team played very solid football. Against Memphis State, Brett broke his own record once again by throwing for 345 yards as he completed 24 of 41 passes. The Eagles won, 31–7. But the club would lose twice more before the season ended, one of the defeats coming at the hands of an always tough Alabama team. The Crimson Tide whipped Southern Miss, 37–14. Even in defeat, however, Brett threw for 300 yards, completing 18 of 41 passes.

The Golden Eagles had a 4–6 record going into their final game, with East Carolina. Despite Brett's heroics, it had been a disappointing season. So everyone just let it all out in the finale. Brett was brilliant all afternoon. He shredded the East Carolina defense to the tune of a career best 26 completions in 35 attempts for 286 yards and 3 touchdowns. Southern Miss won a shootout, 41–27, to finish the year at 5–6.

As for Brett, his numbers continued to impress. In 1989 he had completed 206 passes in 381 attempts for 2,588 yards. He threw for 14 touchdowns and had 10 passes picked off. The reason for the increase in interceptions over the previous year was that the club had to play from behind so often that Brett was forced to take more chances. That meant the defenses knew he was going to throw and were ready.

Though Brett didn't make any of the postseason All-America teams, his throwing arm had already caught the eye of some National Football League scouts. They felt he had potential, but most wanted to see him play out his senior year before they decided how good he could be. The people at Southern Miss were already touting him as a possible candidate for the Heisman Trophy, the award given annually to the college player judged to be the best in the land. Brett, however, wasn't thinking about awards. He just wanted to make sure he and his teammates produced a winning season.

That spring he continued his studies as a special education major and underwent some minor surgery on his throwing elbow. When the semester ended, he returned to Kiln to spend time with his family and have some fun. Little did he know that perhaps the biggest test of his toughness and will was just around the corner.

Brett probably wasn't thinking much about football on July 14, 1990. He had driven out to a place called Ship Island to catch some sun and have fun with his friends. Early that evening Brett was driving home alone in his Nissan Maxima and was just a mile from his house when it happened. An oncoming car failed to dim its lights. Brett was momentarily blinded and swerved his car, fearing he might collide with the other vehicle.

The Nissan hit the shoulder, lurched back onto some loose gravel, and flipped into the air. It then rolled several times before hitting a tree. Scott Favre, who was driving his own car right behind Brett, witnessed the accident firsthand. He said Brett's car flipped so high "you could have driven a dump truck underneath."

Scott stopped his car and ran to his brother's

aid. The wreck of the Nissan was so twisted and mangled that Scott couldn't get the doors open. He had to break the front window with a golf club so he could pull Brett out. He knew immediately that his brother was badly hurt. He asked someone to call an ambulance to rush Brett to the hospital.

Brett was placed in intensive care, and his entire family rushed to his bedside. His injuries were serious but not life-threatening. He had a concussion, a bruised liver, a cracked vertebra, and many scrapes and lacerations. A CAT scan of his brain showed no serious head injury. There was no reason to think he wouldn't make a full recovery. He was very lucky.

"It was very scary right after the crash," his mother said. "People who saw how the car was wrapped around the tree couldn't believe Brett got out alive."

The accident had occurred on a Saturday. By the following Tuesday Brett was out of bed and walking. His thoughts immediately turned to football, and he predicted he would rejoin his Southern Mississippi teammates when practice began on August 13.

"I'm bruised and sore," Brett said, "but I don't have any broken bones. I'll be back. I'll be ready for the first game."

Everyone at Southern Mississippi breathed a sigh of relief. They would have their senior quarterback in the fold. Brett's family, too, was thankful he wasn't more seriously injured. Brett was released from the hospital on July 22, eight days after the accident. His doctors were concerned that Brett's high tolerance for pain might cause him to ignore symptoms that might indicate his injuries weren't fully healed.

Brett, however, had put the accident behind him and was again thinking about football. "The coaches are sending me a playbook this week," he said. "So I'll be studying the plays and getting ready for practice."

But as the days passed, Brett began to realize he wasn't making as much progress as he'd expected.

"When I got out of the hospital I had soreness in my stomach muscles," he said. "I thought I had been bruised by the seat belt during the accident. The doctors even said the soreness should go away. But I wasn't eating much, and when I did, I was throwing up. Then the soreness turned into abdominal pains, and they began getting worse. Finally I went back to the hospital, and the doctors found I had a major intestinal problem."

Brett's stomach injury had apparently caused an intestinal blockage that restricted the flow of blood to the small intestine. As Brett himself put it, "They found that a lot of my intestines had died." The only recourse was surgery, and on August 8, Brett underwent a ninety-minute operation in which a 30-inch portion of his small intestine was removed. It was serious surgery, but fortunately the doctors said Brett should be fine. Once he recovered he would be able to resume his football career.

The car accident was certainly a harrowing experience for Brett, his family, his teammates, and his many fans. Perhaps he realized then just how tenuous a football career could be. Many athletes see their careers shortened or ended by injuries, and Brett's almost ended because another driver failed to dim his headlights.

After that he pursued his sport with increased zeal and intensity. He wanted to make the most of every game. That meant playing to his full potential and winning. It also meant not coming out of a game no matter how many times he was knocked down or how hard he was hit.

Brett Favre was about to begin a journey that would take him to the top.

Chapter 4

The Comeback Kid and the NFL Draft

Shortly after Brett's surgery, his doctors held a press conference. They explained the nature of the surgery, then said that because they had needed only to make a fairly small incision, Brett's recovery would be relatively fast. It was estimated that he could begin working out in three to five weeks. He would probably be ready for full workouts with no restrictions in five or six weeks.

With that projection, it was also estimated that Brett would be able to rejoin his teammates by Southern Mississippi's third game, a September 15 meeting with Georgia. But that didn't mean it would be easy. Brett had lost a great deal of weight and hadn't been able to eat a lot in the weeks after the surgery, while his intestines were healing. In fact, he had lost some 30 pounds by the time he rejoined his teammates.

"It's been a very rough time for Brett," said his coach, Curley Hallman. "First elbow surgery in the spring, then the car wreck and the complications from that. But knowing Brett, I'm sure he'll do everything possible to rehabilitate himself as quickly and completely as possible."

Brett's accident, however, had changed some things. For one, he would probably miss the first couple of games of the season. So the team would have to open up with another quarterback, which would alter the game plan. In Brett, Southern Miss had its most dynamic and talented player in many years. The school had planned to mount a serious campaign, championing Brett as a legitimate Heisman Trophy candidate. If his numbers equaled or surpassed those of his previous two seasons and if the team won big again, the Heisman wasn't totally out of reach.

After Brett's accident, however, the school called off the Heisman hype. That, of course, would take some of the national focus away from Hattiesburg and the Golden Eagles . . . and away from Brett. A number of NFL scouts had seen Brett in action, and all of them were impressed by his arm and his ability to make big plays. But the accident, his injuries, the subsequent surgery, and the missed playing time couldn't possibly enhance his standing with the scouts. By that time, Brett had designs on an NFL career—in fact, it was his ultimate dream.

"After my junior year I already had a pretty good idea about how I stacked up against other quarterbacks at the collegiate level. I could see I had a chance to play in the pros. But after the accident I couldn't help wondering what would happen to my dream."

Brett was still underweight and weak when he began practicing with the team. He worked as hard as he could—harder than he could, sometimes—but his progress was slow. He just wasn't gaining weight or regaining his strength quickly enough. For a while he was really discouraged.

"Four or five days before our opener against Delta State, Brett still didn't look like he'd be able to play for months," said assistant coach Thamus Coleman. "He was weak and he didn't have near his normal velocity on the ball."

There was even talk about redshirting Brett. If he didn't play all year, he would retain another year of eligibility. But Brett would have none of that talk. He wanted to rejoin his teammates as soon as he could, then get on with the business of playing quarterback. To sit out a year was unthinkable, out of the question.

Brett wasn't in uniform when the Golden Eagles opened the 1990 season against Delta State. Fortunately, Delta didn't have a strong team. Southern Miss won the game, 12–0, but without their offensive leader they looked flat and unimpressive.

The following week, they had to play powerful Alabama. The Crimson Tide, which held a 24–3 all-time advantage over the Golden Eagles, was coming in with a typically strong team. Even with Brett, 'Bama would be the heavy favorite. Without him they were off the board.

As soon as the team began practicing for Alabama, Brett surprised everyone by insisting he wanted to play—he was going to play. Brett's declaration came as a surprise to the coaches, doctors, and even his family. Everyone began communicating. His doctors discussed the situation with his father and his coaches. According to his doctors, Brett was medically fit to play. He had healed well from his surgery and could absorb the normal punishment of a football game. The only drawback was that he still hadn't regained his full strength and stamina. The doctors and Brett's family agreed to leave the decision to the coaching staff.

Alabama would be more pumped than usual for the game. The Crimson Tide had a new head coach in Gene Stallings, who had coached in the NFL and was a protégé of Alabama's legendary coach, Paul "Bear" Bryant. Stallings didn't want to lose his first game, and his players vowed to make sure that wouldn't happen. The Southern Miss coaches knew they didn't have a chance without Brett. With him, they might keep it close, at least for a while.

Coach Hallman waited until the morning of the game to make a decision. Brett was in uniform and ready. Freshman John Whitcomb had started the week before against Delta State, but he was very short on experience. Hallman weighed all the possibilities and finally made his choice. It was based on ability, of course, but also on the intangibles—the things you can't see—that the great ones bring to a game. For these reasons, the coach decided to start Brett Favre.

Because Brett wasn't at full strength, the Golden Eagles had decided to run the ball as much as possible. They didn't want to risk Brett's getting hit too often, especially early in the game. They also spotted him with John Whitcomb for several series in the second and third quarters. They wanted him as strong as possible for the final session.

'Bama had a strong offense and rolled up a ton of yards (442), but the Golden Eagles defense made a number of big plays, stopping drives and coming up big whenever necessary. Amazingly, the score was tied at 24–24 with time winding down in the fourth quarter. Southern Miss had the ball deep in its own territory. If they didn't get a couple of first downs, Alabama would get the ball in good field position to go for the victory.

Brett sucked it up and made several key throws for first downs. When the drive finally bogged down at the Alabama 35, Coach Hallman decided to try a long field goal. Add 7 yards for the snap and kick, 10 yards through the end zone to the goalposts, and it would be a 52-yard field goal attempt. Kicker Jim Taylor would be booting into the wind, but with just 3:35 left, it was the only alternative.

The two teams lined up. The ball was snapped and placed down. Taylor stepped into it and booted it as hard as he could. It was high and long . . . and good! The Golden Eagles swarmed around Taylor, celebrating on the field. They now had the lead at 27–24. But the defense had one more job to do: make sure Alabama didn't drive downfield for a score or tying 3-pointer. And that's just what the

Golden Eagle defense did. Southern Miss won the game in an incredible upset.

Brett had completed just 9 of 17 passes for 125 yards. Despite being exhausted, he stood his ground against the Crimson Tide pass rush and made the big throws when he had to.

"I didn't feel any pain out there," Brett said after the game. "But I really got tired."

That was probably an understatement. Brett had given his club every ounce of strength he had. It was his effort that had everyone talking.

"There was no way Brett was in any kind of condition to make a great impact throwing the ball or doing the things he usually did," said Southern Miss sports information director Regiel Napier. "But the difference was simply that he was on the field. The inspiration he brought lifted the whole team up a foot off the ground. They all must have felt that if Brett could go out there, they could all summon a little extra to win the game."

Thamus Coleman also cited Brett's courage as a rallying point for the team. "What he couldn't do with his arm, he did with his leadership," Coleman said. "I know the rest of the guys just said, 'We can't let Brett down.' That's the effect he had."

Even Gene Stallings, unhappy over losing his first game as Alambama coach, couldn't help but admire the way Brett Favre had played under the circumstances. "You can call it a miracle or a legend or whatever you want," Stallings said. "I just know that on that day Brett Favre was larger than life."

It might have been a miracle game, but that

didn't mean it would be a miracle season. The car accident and subsequent surgery had simply sapped too much of Brett's strength and physical condition. Yet Brett played every game for the remainder of the season, continuing to do his best but probably taking a more conservative approach than he would have liked.

So a look at the 1990 numbers quickly shows that Brett's stats didn't equal those of his previous two seasons. His ten best passing games (in yardage) all took place during his first three seasons. He simply didn't throw the football as much during his senior year. The offensive line, in turn, had to be more conservative and selective in order to protect him. Still, his leadership and winning spirit helped propel the Golden Eagles to a successful season.

Coming into the final regular season game, Southern Miss had a 7–3 mark. Their final opponent would be their toughest since the opener against Alabama. They would be meeting the fifteenth-ranked Tigers of Auburn University. A victory would enable the Golden Eagles to realize their dream of defeating both Alabama and Auburn in the same season, and it would also put them squarely in line for a postseason bowl bid. So this game loomed very large. It was played before more than 85,000 fans at Auburn's huge Jordan-Hare Stadium, with most of the fans rooting for the Tigers.

For the first three quarters Auburn controlled the game. The Southern Miss defense played gallantly, holding the Tigers to just 12 points on 4 field goals. But Brett and his offense couldn't crack the Auburn defense. Brett had led his club to three comeback victories during the season, however, so nobody gave up on him.

Early in the final period Brett began driving his team from its own 31-yard line. He mixed running plays with short and medium passes that found their mark. From the 10-yard line he dropped back and fired a touchdown stike to Michael Jackson, completing a 69-yard drive and bringing his team back into the game. The extra point made it 12–7. All Brett wanted now was for his defense to hold so he could get a chance to win it.

Once again he inspired his teammates to greater effort. The defense held Auburn several times. After the last stop deep in Auburn territory, the Tigers had to punt. A 14-yard return gave Brett and his teammates the ball at the Auburn 42-yard line. As usual, Brett had little time, but he made the most of it. He threw sideline passes to stop the clock and march his team downfield. Once again the ball was resting on the 10-yard line with less than a minute left.

Brett came to the line and called signals. He checked out the Auburn defense, then took the snap. He quickly retreated and looked into the end zone. After waiting until the last second, he whipped the ball to tight end Anthony Harris, who hugged it for a touchdown with just 46 seconds left. The point was missed, but that didn't matter. Southern Mississippi had won the game, 13–12.

"Brett did a great job staying with me and waiting until he thought I was open," Harris said.

"Then he put the ball right in there, and I watched it all the way in."

For Brett, it was not only one of the biggest wins of the year but his best game. He had completed 24 of 40 passes for 207 yards and two clutch touchdowns. He was overjoyed.

"This has to be the biggest win I've ever been part of," he said. "We've beaten two of the top teams in the country, and we had to play them at their places both times in front of sellout crowds."

Shortly after the game, Southern Miss learned it had been chosen to play North Carolina State in the All-American Bowl at Birmingham, Alabama. Then, before the bowl game, Coach Hallman resigned to take the head-coaching job at Louisiana State. Southern Miss called upon former offensive coordinator Jeff Bower to be its next coach. Bower had left several years earlier to coach at Oklahoma State. Now he would get to coach Brett for one game, Brett's last as a collegian.

"I told Brett right away that we were going to open it up against N.C. State and go for it all," Bower said. "If I was only going to have him for one game, I made up my mind we'd be throwing the football everywhere but into the press box. I knew it was really rough on the kids, losing their coach so suddenly and having to work with a new staff. Our only chance was if Brett went wild."

The game was a wide-open affair with both teams going for broke. It was certainly an entertaining game, although the outcome left something to be desired. Brett played very well, but the Golden Eagles defense, which had been so gallant for much of the year, couldn't do it one more time. N.C. State won the game, 31–27. Brett Favre's college career was over.

In many ways, what Brett accomplished in 1990 was remarkable. He wasn't expected to play until the team's fourth game. Yet there he was the second week, engineering that great upset over Alabama. When it was over, he did admit that he hadn't been physically right for most of the year.

"I wasn't myself, physically, until the very end," he said. "By the time we played Auburn and North Carolina State, I had my strength back, and we could do some of the things we'd done before. But early in the year, maybe I should have been resting in my room. From a team standpoint, though, it had to be considered a good year, and football *is* a team game."

Brett's numbers didn't reflect the excellent quarterback he had become. In 1990 he was successful on 150 of 275 passes for a 54.5 completion percentage. He threw for just 7 touchdowns, however, and was intercepted six times. There was, of course, a good reason for the drop in numbers, but this drop took national attention away from him and lowered his status with the pro scouts. Still, he would leave Southern Mississippi as the school's all-time leader in completions (613), attempts (1,169), touchdown passes (52), passing yards (7,695), and a number of other records.

Not bad for a kid who received a scholarhip at the last minute and was expected to be a defensive back, at best. But the question now was what would happen next? Brett knew that the elbow surgery, followed by the car accident had caused his stock to drop among NFL scouts.

"I didn't know what to think [about being drafted by the NFL]," he said. "I guess all I could hope was that the scouts would go by what I could do when I was healthy instead of worrying about how I looked when I wasn't. I had to believe that somebody in the NFL would look at my sophomore and junior years, and then maybe at the end of the last year, and make their judgment on that."

Then the old Favre confidence surfaced. "I still believed by then that I could make it big in the NFL. I had to wait and see if somebody in the league agreed with me."

One of those who agreed with Brett was Jeff Bower. Bower had been Brett's offensive coordinator when he started putting up big numbers as a sophomore, then had returned to see him play his final game. That was more than enough for him to judge.

"Brett simply has what it takes," Bower said. "Nothing intimidates him at all. The bigger the game, the better he is. He gives you a chance every time you take the field. He was always an equalizer for us. He made everyone around him better. As far as I'm concerned, they haven't made a level of football where Brett Favre isn't going to be a star."

Brett knew that he still had to showcase his talents for the NFL people. He was hoping to play in both the Senior Bowl and the East-West Shrine Game. These are all-star games held shortly after the bowl games with the purpose of showcasing top college stars for NFL scouts.

One NFL talent evaluator who had an eye on Brett was Ron Wolf, then director of player personnel for the New York Jets. Wolf already knew how much the coaches at Southern Miss loved Brett. He had heard about Brett's being an inspirational leader and winner, but when he received the first set of tapes from Southern Miss he was disappointed.

"They were games from his senior season, and it just wasn't anything really special," Wolf said. "It was apparent he could play, but this was a guy who had been talked about as a first-round pick. With somebody like that, you're looking for him to jump right off the screen at you."

Fortunately, Ron Wolf visited Hattiesburg to check out some other prospect. That was when Thamus Coleman suggested Wolf view some tapes from Brett's junior year. He explained how weak Brett had been for most of 1990 and that he had been playing on pure guts. When Wolf watched the additional tapes, he changed his mind, thinking that Brett might be the steal of the upcoming draft. Like other scouts, he was eager to see Brett play in the upcoming Senior Bowl.

That bowl game could have been a disaster for Brett. It was played in Mobile, Alabama, with NFL coaches and assistants handling both teams. Jim Mora of the New Orleans Saints was coaching Brett's team and named him the starting quarterback. During that practice week, Brett spoke with a number of scouts and coaches, and he felt that he was being regarded as a first- or second-round choice.

It was a rainy day at Ladd Stadium and the footing wasn't good. Brett had to face a brutal pass rush all afternoon, and the condition of the field took away some of his quickness. As a result, he was sacked three times and lost a fumble. When he did throw, he completed just 7 of 15 passes for 62 yards, while his teammate, Dan McGwire of San Diego State, who split the QB duties with Brett, completed 11 of 23 tosses for 165 yards and two touchdowns. The team lost, 38–28, and Brett felt he might have lost more than a game.

"Let's face it, I got killed," he said afterward. "It wasn't fun, and I didn't enjoy it. I didn't get the protection that some of the other guys got. All-star games are often pitch-and-catch. For me, it was more a game of getting killed than pitch-and-catch."

He wondered what the scouts and coaches felt now. He felt his only chance to redeem himself would be in the East-West Shrine Game. That game would be played on January 26, a week after the Senior Bowl, at Stanford University in California. Because the games were a week and nearly a continent apart, many of those who played in the Senior Bowl decided to pass up the East-West Shrine Game. Not Brett. He flew to California and began getting ready at once. This would be a final chance for him to show the NFL people what he could do.

Brett had just a few days to get to know his teammates and receivers. Yet when he took the field at Stanford, he was a completely different player from the one who had struggled in the Senior Bowl. He was self-assured and decisive, and his great physical skills were in evidence. He took control of the game from the moment he stepped on the field and made it his special show.

At one point he calmly stepped back and fired a 54-yard touchdown bomb to Alabama receiver Lamonde Russell. Later he led his team on a long drive, then used a pump fake to freeze the defense and ran 7 yards into the end zone for another score. When it was over, Brett had completed 15 of 26 passes for 218 yards and was named co–Offensive Player of the Game. Ron Wolf of the Jets was once again in attendance, and he came away feeling that Brett was the man his team needed.

"Brett completely dominated the day," Wolf said. "He had so many things you look for in a quarterback. He seemed to be a natural leader, a win-at-all-costs player. He had great skill and ability. I walked out of there and told our people that Brett Favre is the best college quarterback in the country. We've got to get him."

There were probably others who coveted Brett. The 1991 NFL draft was set for April. By that time, Wolf had convinced the Jets' general manager, the late Dick Steinberg, that Brett had the talent to develop into a franchise quarterback. If the Jets had a number-one draft choice that year, they would have grabbed Brett, perhaps altering the history of the National Football League. But they had traded away their top pick and wouldn't choose until the second round. So all they could do was hope.

In the first round only two quarterbacks were picked. Todd Marinovich of the University of Southern California was taken by the Los Angeles (now Oakland) Raiders, and Dan McGwire, who had outshone Brett in the Senior Bowl, was tabbed by the Seattle Seahawks. Then the second round began.

The Jets had the thirty-fourth pick overall, which meant that they were still fairly early in the second round. The team failed to make a deal to move up. They could only hope Brett was still available. As it turned out, they missed by a hair. The Atlanta Falcons, picking just ahead of the Jets, surprised a lot of people by making Brett Favre their second-round pick, the thirty-third player taken in the draft and the third quarterback chosen.

Brett was with his family back in Kiln on draft day. He fully expected to be taken by the Jets. In fact, his father remembers the Jets calling minutes before they were ready to choose.

"The Jets had Brett on the telephone before he was selected," Irvin Favre said. "They told him, 'We're going to take you with the next pick.' Well, Brett finally had to get off the phone. Then he learned Atlanta had taken him."

Chapter 5

Becoming a Green Bay Packer

Although Brett was surprised that Atlanta had cut the Jets off at the last second, he wasn't unhappy about it. In fact, he was quite pleased to learn he would be going to Atlanta. After all, he would still be based in his beloved South. The Falcons played the Saints twice each season, and New Orleans was only a short distance from home, so his family and friends would get to see him in action. At first he felt it couldn't have worked out better.

Chris Miller was the Falcons' starting signal caller. Miller was a solid quarterback, but he'd been injured a number of times. In fact, he rarely went through a season without missing some games. Because the Falcons didn't have a solid backup, Brett figured he'd fill that slot. And because of Miller's medical history, Brett's chances of seeing game action as a rookie were good.

Brett went to his first professional training camp with the same enthusiasm he had always shown. He worked hard and felt he was earning his place on the team. All he wanted, as always, was a chance to show his stuff. He was beginning to feel he would get it. His confidence told him he could be an outstanding NFL quarterback. That belief in his own ability had never left him.

But just when Brett felt he had found his niche as a rookie, the Falcons made a move that not only took the heart out of him but also could have put his entire career in jeopardy. They made a trade that brought quarterback Billy Joe Tolliver to the team. Tolliver was a veteran who had never been a regular starter but was considered a more than adequate backup. He was immediately penciled in as number two behind Miller, with Brett becoming third.

"I walked in one day and, boom, I'm third string," Brett recalled. "There was no explanation, no discussion. I knew right then and there that I wouldn't have much of a chance to play, and for somebody who had never sat on the bench his whole life, that was hard to accept. In fact, it just killed me."

It was also the beginning of perhaps the worst period in Brett's football life. He lost his focus, and his attitude changed. Maybe it was simply that he wasn't mature enough to handle this kind of adversity. He simply didn't feel that he was part of the team, and that was the way he acted. Before long, he was pretty deep in Coach Jerry Glanville's doghouse. And he wasn't playing at all.

After Tolliver came in, Brett spoke with offensive coordinator June Jones, asking why he was suddenly number three. "He said they brought Billy in for insurance purposes," Brett recalled, "for experience, and that they just wanted to give me a year to learn and progress. They didn't want to put me in too many situations, as young as I was."

That explanation didn't sit well with Brett. His attitude went from bad to worse.

"I just said the hell with it," Brett would admit later. "I went out every night, gained weight, and was out of shape. I didn't study [the playbook] and didn't care. I'd show up just in time for meetings, and I'd be out of there the second the meetings were over."

Coach Glanville said that Brett even missed some meetings. He referred to him as "the Pillsbury Doughboy" because of his weight gain. The Falcons were in contention for a playoff berth, and Brett was playing absolutely no part in it. He didn't even get to take snaps in practice with the Atlanta offense. Rather, he played for the scout team, giving the first-string defense a chance to get ready for its opponents.

Veteran linebacker Jessie Tuggle remembers Brett using his strong arm to force cannonlike throws into overloaded coverage just to see if he could complete the pass. Ironically, though Brett was being something of a wise guy, Tuggle said that he did it with such strength and cockiness that a lot of the players thought he could be a star someday.

Although Brett had looked impressive at times in the preseason, before Tolliver came aboard, he virtually disappeared once the regular season started. He was active for only three of the team's sixteen games, throwing just five passes and completing not a single one. All the time the Falcons were going 10–6 and making the playoffs.

The team eventually lost to the Washington Redskins in the playoffs, and shortly afterward June Jones told Brett that the team had no plans to move him. They still felt he had a future. Apparently Jerry Glanville didn't agree, however. The Falcons' general manager, Ken Herock, said that Glanville hadn't even wanted the team to draft Brett. And when Brett's attitude crashed, Glanville wanted him gone.

"If your coach is down on a guy like [Glanville] was, you have to move him," Ken Herock said. "But with Brett Favre, you can definitely say 'I did it with reluctance.'"

If the Falcons moved Brett, where would he go? Once again fate took a hand. In November of 1991, shortly after Brett's rookie year began, Ron Wolf left the New York Jets to become the general manager of the Green Bay Packers. Wolf, of course, was still sky-high on Brett. Once he got to Green Bay, he dismissed Lindy Infante as coach and replaced him with Mike Holmgren. Then the two went about rebuilding the team.

When the Packers played the Falcons that year, Wolf watched Brett in warm-ups. He still marveled at the way he threw the football. He remembered how badly he'd wanted Brett when he was with the Jets. Now he felt Brett was the man to help lead the Packers back to the top.

Early in 1992 Ron Wolf began discussing a trade for Brett with the Falcons. Finally Atlanta agreed to ship Brett to the Packers in return for Green Bay's first draft choice in 1992. Even Brett admitted that it must have looked as if the Falcons got the better of the deal. He had done nothing so far, and a number-one draft choice could still make an impact.

It also didn't help Brett's reputation when Jerry Glanville said good-bye by labeling him "uncoachable . . . the kind of kid you would kick out of kindergarten."

None of that mattered now. On February 10, 1992, Brett Favre officially became a Green Bay Packer. As far as he was concerned, 1991 just didn't count. This would be his first year. He was starting fresh.

Brett was now a member of one of the National Football League's old, storied franchises. The Packers had begun play in just the second year of the National Football League's existence. That was back in 1921 when Curly Lambeau, the team's founder, sought financial backing from the Green Bay–based company where he worked. That was the Indian Packing Company, which packed processed meats. The company put up all of $500 to pay for jerseys, pads, pants, and a football. In turn, the team was called the Green Bay Packers.

With Curly Lambeau as their first and longtime coach, the Packers won their first championship in 1929. At that time, the NFL was composed of a single division with the team having the best record being declared champions. The Packers were 12-0-1 that year. They won the next two years as well, compiling marks of 10-3-1 and 12–2. The first Packers superstar was a runner named John McNally. But to football fans, he was known as Johnny Blood, a gridiron name if there ever was one.

In 1933 the league was split into two divisions, and a championship game was created. The Packers remained a top team and won the NFL title in 1936, 1939, and 1944. After that, the team went into a long decline, posting nine losing seasons between 1945 and 1958. Then, in 1959, things changed.

That was the year Vince Lombardi took over as head coach. The team had finished with a dismal 1-10-1 record in 1958. Lombardi, who had been an assistant with the New York Giants, would have none of that. The first time he met with his new team, Lombardi held a ball out in front of him and said, "Gentlemen, this is a football. Before we're done, we're gonna run it down everybody's throat."

Lombardi made good on his word. He immediately weeded out the malingerers, the marginal players, and those who wouldn't adhere to his rules and maxims. During his first season the Packers were winners at 7–5. A year later they were in the championship game, losing to the

Eagles, 17–13. And the following year, the dynasty really began. The Pack was 11–3 in the regular season, then whipped the tough New York Giants, 37–0, in the championship game.

Under Lombardi, the Packers would win five NFL championships and the first two Super Bowls ever played. The small city of Green Bay, Wisconsin, became known as Titletown, USA, and Lombardi became a coaching legend. After the team's second Super Bowl victory following the 1967 season, Lombardi gave up coaching to become the Packers general manager. But he got restless and agreed to coach the Washington Redskins in 1969.

Once again he began working his magic. He took the Skins from a 5–9 team in 1968 to a 7–5 winner in his first year. But a year later Lombardi was stricken with cancer and died soon after. Yet he remains a legend, a Packer legend, and one that subsequent Green Bay teams never seemed to live up to.

Along with the coach, the individual players from those dynasty years always remained in the hearts of Green Bay fans. The years of futility that followed left the loyal fans at Lambeau Field longing for the days of Bart Starr, Paul Hornung, Jim Taylor, Ray Nitschke, Willie Davis, Dave Robinson, Willie Wood, Herb Adderley, and the rest of the Packer immortals.

As the NFL grew and expanded in the 1970s and 1980s, the Packers remained marginal, at best. In fact, from the time Lombardi left after 1967 until Brett Favre and Mike Holmgren came in 1992, the team had fifteen losing seasons and several others in which they were at, or barely over, the .500 mark. The Pack made the playoffs just twice between 1968 and 1991. So by the time Brett arrived, everyone in Green Bay was hungering for a winner.

In 1991 the Packers had another terrible season, finishing with a 4–12 record. It was time for a change, a major one. Ron Wolf took a lot of heat when he traded a top draft choice for Brett. It was his first major move as general manager, and he knew an awful lot was riding on it.

"'Have you lost your mind?' was what most people said to me," Wolf recalled. "But I just really liked [Brett]. He had that unexplainable something about him."

Holmgren—the new coach, who had been an offensive coordinator with the San Francisco 49ers—also knew that much of the team's future success rested with its quarterback. He too felt that Brett had a chance to be an impact player.

"I really didn't know his reputation," Holmgren said, "but I do remember that when I'd scouted him while I was with San Francisco, I wrote in my report, 'This guy is blue collar.' I figured he was a throwback with a personality. And personalities as a rule don't scare me, as long as they're responsible and willing to meet me halfway."

Brett would be in for a big change in joining Green Bay. All his life he had lived and played in the South, where the weather is warm year-round. Green Bay, Wisconsin, was in the North, where the weather was not only cold but sometimes absolutely frigid. Lambeau Field in December and

January was often referred to as "the frozen tundra." Many teams used to playing in warmer weather came to Green Bay and fell victim to the elements as much as to the Packers. That was something Brett would have to deal with in making the transition to his new team.

The starting quarterback in 1992 was veteran Don Majkowski. He had put together an outstanding season back in 1989 when the Pack finished a surprising 10–6 and missed the NFC Central Division title by virtue of a tie with the 10–6 Minnesota Vikings. Majkowski was so good that year that he earned the nickname "the Majik Man."

But Majkowski also had a history of getting hurt. In 1990 and 1991 he missed fourteen full games and parts of five others as his team floundered. So while Majkowski was named the starter for 1992, Brett knew he would have to be ready as backup. Getting ready wasn't as easy as it sounded.

During his tenure as a quarterback coach and offensive coordinator, Holmgren had compiled quite a playbook. When he took over the Packers, he brought with him more than a thousand plays and installed a sophisticated passing scheme that was not easy to learn. Brett had to work harder than he ever had. No more partying the way he had in Atlanta. As the primary backup to an injury-prone starter, he knew he had to be ready at a moment's notice.

Brett had grown into a solid 6-foot-2-inch, 220-pound quarterback who was tough as nails and felt he could handle anything on the football field. As always, one of his biggest boosters was his father.

"Brett wants to win very badly," Irvin Favre said. "He's the most hardheaded of my sons. He's mean. He's rawboned. He's a battler."

The Packers opened the 1992 season against their division rival, the Minnesota Vikings. Majkowski was at the helm for the entire game, and the Packers lost. A week later the Pack went up against the Tampa Bay Buccaneers. The Bucs jumped on top quickly, with Majkowski and the offense not producing a single point in the first half. Tampa Bay went to the locker room with a 17–0 lead. Then, when the third quarter began, there was a surprise change. Majkowski was on the bench, and Brett Favre was in the game at quarterback.

It was Brett's first real taste of NFL action, and he didn't do badly. He completed 8 of 14 passes for 73 yards. The offense produced just a single field goal, and the team lost big, 31–3. Brett had also thrown an interception and been sacked four times, but at least he had gotten his feet wet. Coach Holmgren made it clear, however, that Majkowski was still his starting quarterback.

After the game Majkowski said he was unhappy with the switch. Like any competitor, he had wanted to stay in the game. Coach Holmgren tried to avoid any quarterback controversy.

"Some bad things happened in the first half, and they weren't Don's [Majkowski's] fault," Holmgren said. "Because of the way the game was going, I said what the heck. I wanted to play Brett sometime this season. Early in the season."

As for Brett, the taste of real NFL action only

made him hunger for more. And he wouldn't be happy waiting.

"I really want to play now," Brett said. "Sitting is easier when you haven't gotten in a game. You're almost willing to wait for your time to come. But now I've had a chance to play, and I want to get back in. It's tough, because I'm chomping at the bit."

Chapter 6

Taking Over the Offense

The third game of the season was at Lambeau Field against the Cincinnati Bengals. As Coach Holmgren had promised, Majkowski was back as starter. That left Brett where he didn't want to be—on the sidelines. A second-string quarterback never hopes that the man ahead of him will get hurt, because he wants the job on his own merit. And it's best for the team if the two quarterbacks work together. Sometimes one will see a way to help the other.

But Brett Favre had the itch. He wanted to play very badly. The action he'd had against Tampa Bay served to whet his appetite. Playing was fun again. It was competitive. Action was something he hadn't had during his lost season with the Falcons—and it was something he wanted again, as soon as possible.

Brett didn't have long to wait. In the first quarter of the Bengals game, Majkowski was hit hard. When the players unstacked, the quarterback remained on the turf. When he was helped to his feet he was limping badly. Coach Holmgren barked at Brett to warm up as Majkowski was helped from the field. Less than a month before his twenty-third birthday, Brett Favre became the quarterback of the Green Bay Packers.

It took him a while to gain confidence. He was throwing well, but the team couldn't sustain their drives. Fortunately, the defense kept them in the game, but at the beginning of the fourth and final period the Packers trailed the Bengals by a score of 17–3. Then, without warning, Brett Favre got the Packers offense moving.

He drove the team downfield and threw his first NFL touchdown pass, making it a 17–10 game. Cincy then came back to kick a field goal before another Favre drive led to a second score for the Packers. It was now a 20–17 game, with time running down. Brett had put his team back in it with crisp, sure passes. He looked like anything but a raw rookie—which, essentially, he was.

The game, however, wasn't over. Cincinnati tried to pad its lead and eat up the clock with another drive. When it stalled at the Packers' 24, Cincy's Jim Breech came on and booted a 41-yard field goal. That made the score 23–17. Now there was just 1:07 left, and the Packers had no timeouts. When the Bengals' kickoff left the ball at the 8-yard line, 92 yards from the goal line, no one thought the Packers had a chance.

Fortunately, Brett Favre didn't feel that way. He worked the clock like a seasoned veteran, sticking with sideline passes that would allow the receiver to go out of bounds and stop the clock, which would give his team precious seconds. Yet he moved the Pack relentlessly up the field. Finally, with just 13 seconds left, the ball was on the Cincinnati 35-yard line. There was time for one, maybe two more plays. Brett ducked in over center, looking at the Cincinnati defense.

He took the snap and dropped back as the final seconds began ticking off the clock. Looking downfield, Brett saw wide receiver Kitrick Taylor getting open. With the poise of a veteran, Brett fired a pass toward the end zone. Every eye in Lambeau Field followed the flight of the ball as it soared, then descended into the hands of Kitrick Taylor, who raced with it into the end zone. Touchdown! Brett had done it, brought his team back. His clutch pass with 13 seconds left had tied the game, and the extra point won it, giving the Packers a 24–23 victory.

Brett had been absolutely brilliant. In his first taste of sustained action, he completed 22 of 39 passes for 289 yards and two touchdowns. He had been sacked five times but was smart enough not to be pressured into an interception. It had to be one of the most brilliant debuts for a quarterback ever. Of course, talent usually has to be combined with a little luck.

"What people don't remember about that day is that I should have had six or seven interceptions," the self-effacing Brett said. "I was all over the place."

Brett meant that his passes weren't as accurate as he would have liked. Perfectionists tend to think like that. Sure, he missed some receivers. But the bottom line was that he hit enough to win the game.

What most people didn't know was that Brett was a nervous wreck when he was called on to enter the game. "I was shaky and nervous, knowing what was on the line," he said. "I was the guy. Everybody was counting on me. I felt like I was going to be sick. Thank God I held on until after the game."

After the game the Packers learned that Majkowski would be out for two to four weeks. That meant Brett would be starting the following week against the always tough Pittsburgh Steelers. He might have several more starts as well, a real chance to establish himself. Once Majkowski recovered, the coaches would have to decide which quarterback would run the team.

The game plan against Pittsburgh called for Brett to be more conservative. He threw the football just 19 times, completing 14 for 210 yards and two touchdowns. One of them was a 76-yard bomb to wide receiver Sterling Sharpe that gave the Packers a 10–3 halftime lead.

The Packers didn't put the game away until the fourth quarter. Early in the period they had the ball at the Pittsburgh 8-yard line. Coach Holmgren called a play in which rookie wide receiver Robert

Brooks would fake a slant-in, then fade toward the right corner of the end zone.

"Remember," the coach told his quarterback. "You've really got to like it to throw it. It has to be there."

In other words, even though that was the play, Brett had to see it happening, feel he could complete the pass before throwing it. It was a decision a quarterback had to make in a split second. Brett went out, took the snap, pump-faked to Brooks on the slant-in, and then waited another second before floating the ball to Brooks in the right side of the end zone. That score gave the Packers a 17–3 victory and evened their record at 2–2.

Later Holmgren explained why he had told Brett he had to like it to throw it. "I had to tell him that, because Brett has a wild hair. Last week, after the euphoria of our win, I congratulated him and then told him he'd made mistakes on twenty-five plays. I told him if we had lost, the quarterback would have been the reason."

There was a mixed message in what the coach said to Brett. Holmgren had cut his teeth on the so-called West Coast offense, popularized by Coach Bill Walsh, quarterback Joe Montana, and the highly successful San Francisco 49ers. It was a tight-knit offense, carefully controlled by the coach and offensive coordinator, designed to exploit a defense and break it down, while moving the football with short and medium-range passes. The game plan and much of the passing attack were carefully choreographed in advance.

Brett was more of a let-it-all-hang-out quarterback. He was a freewheeling improviser who had complete faith in his arm and a tendency to make something out of nothing. While Holmgren recognized Brett's great talent, he wondered if the quarterback had enough discipline to carry out his offensive scheme. This was just the first skirmish in what would become a battle of wills for the next several years.

But despite his reservations about Brett, Coach Holmgren knew the Packers had responded to Brett in a way they hadn't to Don Majkowski. It wasn't a knock on Majkowski as much as a vote of confidence for the charisma that Brett brought with him. Without waiting for Majkowski's injury to heal, Coach Holmgren named Brett the starting quarterback for the remainder of the season.

That decision marked an incredible turnaround. A year earlier Brett had been languishing as a third-stringer with the Falcons. His attitude wasn't good. He didn't feel that he was part of the team, and he allowed himself to gain weight and lose conditioning. His coach was ripping him constantly, and his future looked bleak. A year later, that same quarterback, with a new team and a new coach, would be starting the final twelve games of the season. He was being thrown into a complex offense with no experience—not easy for a kid who was not yet twenty-three years old.

It wouldn't be all smooth sailing for him. The following week the Pack traveled to Atlanta to face the Falcons. If Brett wanted to show off his skills to any team, it would be the Falcons. He played well, completing 33 of 43 passes for 276 yards, one TD, and one interception. He had completed an amazing 76.7 percent of his passes. It was a great game—except for one thing: the Packers lost.

Two more losses followed, to Cleveland and Chicago, though Brett was still putting good numbers on the board. The quarterback, of course, can't do the job alone, and the Packers were still far from a complete team. After all, the season before, they had checked out with a 4–12 record. Before the season, most of the experts had felt that a .500 season would be a stretch but a solid improvement. But now the team stood at 2–5. A couple more losses and the Packers would be in real trouble.

Coach Holmgren stayed with Brett, and the Pack bounced back to top the Lions, with Brett hitting 22 of 37 passes and throwing for a pair of scores. A loss to the New York Giants followed. Although Brett passed for 279 yards, he was intercepted three times. He had been picked off only three times all year going into that game. This time the mistakes hurt. Brett showed he wasn't afraid to put his body on the line when he tackled Giants' linebacker Pepper Johnson following one of the intercepts.

The following week the Packers hosted the Philadelphia Eagles at Lambeau. The game was a turning point and showed the team just what kind of a competitor they had as their quarterback. When the Packers had the ball during the first quarter, the Eagles went after Brett with a blitz. All-Pro defensive end Reggie White hit Brett from the blind side and drove him hard to the turf. Brett got up and headed to the sideline, his left shoulder apparently injured.

On the sideline, it was determined that Brett had suffered a first-degree separation of his left shoulder. It wasn't his throwing side, but it was an extremely painful injury. Most quarterbacks would have come out of the game. Not Brett. Despite intense pain, he wasn't about to give up.

"I saw Don Majkowski rarin' to go, and if he'd gotten back in there, I might never have gotten my spot back," Brett said afterward.

He returned to the field to a standing ovation the next time the Packers had the ball. He had waited too long for his chance to let any injury stop him. Although he played well in the second quarter, Brett continued to be in intense pain. He couldn't lift his arm as high as his shoulder and couldn't hand off to the left. At halftime, the doctors and coaches again asked if he wanted to come out.

"The doctors said, 'It's your choice, but we can shoot it up [with Novocain to deaden the pain] without further injury.' I said, 'Let's do it.' They had to pull my shoulder out, and they stuck the needle way down in my shoulder. In a little while I didn't feel any pain."

Brett went on to have a brilliant second half, once again bringing the Packers back in the fourth quarter. He overcame a 24–21 deficit to lead the Pack to a 27–24 upset victory over the playoff-bound Eagles. On that afternoon he connected with 23 of 33 passes for 275 yards and two scores. He was picked off twice, but overcame the mistakes to prevail. And he overcame the pain to win the respect and admiration of the coaches and his teammates. They knew they had a real gamer at quarterback.

Brett had seen Majkowski lose his job to injury, and he didn't want the same thing to happen to him. He loved playing too much. He also felt the team was on the brink of making some real progress. His sense of responsibility to his teammates, coaches, and fans helped keep in him there. And he was right: following the Philly game, the team went on a real roll.

With Brett at the helm, the Pack won five more games, running the winning streak to six. They toppled the Bears, Tampa Bay, Detroit, Houston, and the Rams. In those five victories Brett threw 8 scoring passes and was picked off only twice. Against the Lions he connected on 15 of 19 passes, an impressive 78.9 completion rate. He also threw for 3 scores in that one, including a 65-yarder to Sterling Sharpe as the Pack won, 38–10. For a young kid playing his first full year, he was doing amazing things.

Despite a season-ending loss to Minnesota, the Packers had surprised everyone by finishing at 9–7. They didn't make the playoffs, but they looked like contenders in the near future. As for Brett Favre, he had put together a thoroughly amazing season. His numbers weren't those normally compiled by a quarterback being thrown to the NFL wolves for the first time.

He had completed 302 of 471 passes for 3,227 yards and a 64.1 completion percentage. He threw for 18 touchdowns with 13 passes picked off. His 85.3 quarterback rating placed him fifth in the NFC and sixth in the entire NFL. In fact, he had a better quarterback rating than such established stars as Dan Marino, Jim Kelly, John Elway, and Boomer Esiason. This wasn't all. . . .

Brett had led the Packers to their second-best record in twenty years. He also set a team record for the highest completion percentage for a season and for the most consecutive 200-yard passing games. He went over that mark eleven straight times. His 302 completions tied him with those of the Cowboys' Troy Aikman for most in the NFC, and he had the third-lowest interception percentage (2.76) of all NFL quarterbacks.

That still wasn't all. Brett was named as the third quarterback for the NFC in the annual postseason Pro Bowl game. Just twenty-three years old, he became the youngest quarterback ever to play in the Pro Bowl.

"If Brett can stay healthy," Coach Holmgren said, "he will be the cornerstone of our football team for many years to come."

Brett was extremely pleased with his play in the 1992 season. But despite the numbers, he knew he had a long way to go to master Coach Holmgren's total passing attack.

"In the first year or so I don't think anybody on our team knew exactly what we were doing," Brett said, looking back. He admitted he had problems picking up secondary receivers and often took off and ran if his primary receiver was covered. He did that 47 times, picking up 198 yards for a 4.2 average. So he wasn't a bad runner, either.

He also had a superstar receiver in Sterling Sharpe, who led the entire NFL with 108 catches for 1,461 yards and 13 touchdowns. But the Packers lacked a franchise running back and the defense was still spotty. Favre and the offense had put 276 points on the board, but the defense allowed 296 points. They were the only team in the NFL with a winning record that allowed more points than they scored.

Brett proved one other thing in 1992: that the quarterback from the Deep South could perform in cold weather. The Packers played four home games in which the temperature was below 35 degrees, and they won them all. They played the Rams on December 20 on a frigid, 8-degree day, and Brett performed very well. In fact, his perfect cold-weather record would continue to stand in upcoming years. Seems he had taken to the frigid air the way polar bears take to ice.

So while the team still had to upgrade its personnel in a few areas, one of the positions that seemed set was quarterback. By all appearances, Brett Favre was there to stay . . . for a long time.

Chapter 7

The Road Gets Rocky

Brett received a boatload of praise for his play in 1992. Many were already predicting that he would become the next great quarterback in the NFL. In fact, a number of Johnny-come-latelies were saying they had seen Brett at Southern Mississippi or in the East-West game and had known all along that he would be great. He still had a long way to go, though. One season does not a career make. Coach Holmgren knew Brett had the potential, but he needed to fulfill it.

"If you settle for playing it safe in this business, you'll never be better than average," he explained. "Then pretty soon you're gone. Our goal isn't to be mediocre. It's to win a Super Bowl. And to do that, in our offense we needed a big-time quarterback. We didn't mind getting one we had to teach. That's probably the best situation, anyway, finding somebody with the right tools and molding the guy yourself."

The question soon after the 1993 season began was whether Brett Favre could be molded. He was a free spirit, the kind of quarterback who had always wanted to do it his way. Yet in the season opener against the L.A. Rams, Brett looked as solid as ever. He completed 19 of 29 passes for 264 yards and 2 scores as the Pack won the game in impressive fashion, 36–6.

In addition to Brett and the offense, the defense had been bolstered by the addition of defensive end Reggie White. White was already considered an all-time great when he joined the Packers from the Eagles via free agency. The player known as the Minister of Defense was the same Reggie White who had separated Brett's shoulder the season before. Now they were teammates with a common goal: to win.

So after week one, optimism abounded. But then something happened. Brett and the offense didn't look sharp for three games, as the Pack lost to Philadelphia, Minnesota, and powerful Dallas. Against Philly, Brett threw for just 111 yards, his lowest total since becoming a starter. During the next two weeks he passed for 150 and 174 yards respectively. This was a far cry from his passing a year earlier, when he was over the 200-yard passing mark in 11 straight games. It was at this point that Brett and Coach Holmgren began to clash on the execution of the passing game.

Basically, Holmgren wanted Brett to stay within the offense. Brett, however, had a penchant for taking chances, for improvising whenever *he* felt it was the best move. The coach knew that all quarterbacks must sometimes improvise; there is such a thing as a broken play, when the quarterback is on his own. But Holmgren felt that Brett anticipated being on his own. Both men wanted control, but they had to meet in the middle if the team was to reach its ultimate goal.

Nothing, however, quiets a controversy as much as a series of wins. So when the Pack won six of their next seven games, things cooled down between player and coach. The team was now 7–4 and still in the running for a playoff berth. Brett had some big games during the streak. He threw for 268 yards and 4 touchdowns in a victory over Tampa Bay and completed 24 of 33 passes (72.7 percent) in a win over the Lions. Even in a loss that ended the run, he threw for 402 yards and 2 scores against the Bears.

In that game, however, Brett was intercepted three times. That was one of the big differences between 1992 and 1993. Brett's passes were being picked off at an alarming rate. Even at Southern Mississippi he'd always had an outstanding interception rate. He simply didn't throw the ball into the wrong hands very often. Yet after twelve games, Brett had thrown for fifteen touchdowns and had been picked off eighteen times.

The win-one, lose-one pattern was to continue for the rest of the year. After a victory over San Diego, the Pack lost to Minnesota. They bounced back to beat the Raiders but, in the season finale, were beaten by Detroit. Brett was picked off four times.

For the second straight year the Packers finished at 9–7, the difference this time being that the team made the playoffs as a wild card. Brett started all 16 games and completed 318 of 522 passes for 3,303 yards, a 60.9 completion percentage. But his 19 touchdown passes were topped by his 24 interceptions, and that helped to drop his final quarterback efficiency rating to 72.2, down from 85.3 the previous season.

Before the playoffs began, Brett and his coach clashed again. Brett had apparently said in an interview that he wasn't going to change his style, that the team was being successful with his risk-taking on the field. He implied that he thought the team would be better off if he continued to play the game his way.

Holmgren was livid when he saw the remarks. He chastised Brett for his tendency to run around the field and throw "stupid interceptions." Brett, of course, always defended his way.

"He would say things like 'Hey, we were 9–7 and made the playoffs. That's a pretty good year,'" Holmgren explained. "And I'd ask him if he wanted to be 9–7 his whole life. I didn't want to be 9–7 my whole life. 'We want to win the Super Bowl here,' I said. I told him that if he didn't learn more and more about this offense, and run it the way he was supposed to, I didn't care how many spectacular plays he made every once in a while. I told him he'd always be a 9–7 quarterback.

"We had a pretty heated exchange," the coach continued. "I think deep down Brett knew I was right. Here was a guy with all this talent, and if he applied himself properly and executed things in the right framework, maybe we're going to get to the Super Bowl. But playing like a kid on the street? No way."

Brett, of course, had come a long way in a short time. He hadn't sat behind an established star and learned slowly. He was well aware of that.

"I got thrown into the toughest offense in the game as a starter at twenty-two," he said. "Every other guy who's played [the West Coast offense] sat for a year or two and learned. Joe Montana sat behind Steve DeBerg. Steve Young sat behind Joe. Steve Bono sat behind both of them. That's why it was frustrating when people would get on me."

In the wild-card playoff game that year, the Packers had to meet division rival Detroit. The Lions had won the NFC Central with a 10–6 mark. The teams had split their two regular-season games, but just a week earlier the Lions had won the season finale from the Pack. The game was played at the SilverDome in Detroit and was close right from the start. The Lions were led by the great running back, Barry Sanders, while the Packers depended more on the Favre-to-Sharpe passing combination. During the regular season, Sharpe had set a new NFL record with 112 receptions. He was definitely a game-breaker.

The game was close into the final quarter. The Lions held a 24–21 lead as the clock ticked down to the final minute. Brett had thrown a pair of touchdown passes to Sharpe and now had the Pack moving again. This time the clock was his biggest foe. With the ball on the Detroit 40-yard line, Brett called signals, took the snap, and dropped back to pass.

The Lions were coming after him, and he had to scramble out of the pocket to avoid a sack. Running to his left, he saw Sterling Sharpe streaking down the right side of the field toward the end. There was no time to set and throw. Using his powerful arm, Brett threw across his body and lofted the ball deep. Sharpe ran under it just as he crossed the goal line. It was an absolutely spectacular throw, the kind many quarterbacks couldn't make, and it put the Packers in the lead. The point after made it 28–24, and that was the way the game ended.

Ironically, the Packers had won it on one of Brett's improvised riverboat-gambler plays. He had completed 15 of 26 passes for 204 yards and 3 touchdowns to put his team into the divisional playoff game against the powerful Dallas Cowboys. Led by quarterback Troy Aikman, running back Emmitt Smith, and wide receiver Michael Irvin, and operating behind a massive offensive line, the Cowboys would be hard to stop. Their defense was as effective as their offense, and they were the favorites to win it all.

The game was played on January 16 at Texas Stadium. If the Packers could win, they would next play for the NFC championship and a trip to the Super Bowl. The first quarter was very physical, with both teams trying to establish dominance.

The Packers scored first on a field goal and held a 3–0 lead as the period ended.

In the second session the power of the Cowboys began to dominate. Quarterback Aikman threw a pair of TD passes, and Eddie Murray kicked a 41-yard field goal. Meanwhile, the Dallas defense put the clamps on Favre and company. At halftime Dallas had a 17–3 lead. In the second half, Brett mounted a comeback, throwing a 2-yard scoring pass to Robert Brooks and a 29-yarder to Sharpe. But the Cowboys had too many weapons on this day and hung on to win it, 27–17.

Brett closed out his second full season by hitting on 28 of 45 passes for 331 yards and two scores. Yet his coach felt he still had a lot to learn. Whether the two would continue to clash in 1994 was an important question. Despite the success of his first two years, and despite a number of spectacular last-second victories, Brett would be judged by the upcoming season. Either he would begin rising to greatness, or he would fall into mediocrity.

The team continued to add solid players to both the offense and the defense. Wideouts Sharpe and Robert Brooks gave Brett a pair of speedy targets, while running back Edgar Bennett was a solid performer in both rushing and receiving. Reggie White and safety Leroy Butler anchored the improving defense, and everyone hoped this would be the Pack's breakthrough year.

By this time Brett was working with quarterback coach Steve Mariucci, who acted almost as a

A great quarterback at the top of his game, with the confident look of a winner. *(Vernon J. Biever)*

Brett was so outstanding during his junior year at Southern Mississippi that he was being touted as a future Heisman Trophy candidate. *(Courtesy of University of Southern Mississippi)*

When he decides to run, Favre can be punishing. Here he barrels into the end zone in a 1997 game against the Rams. *(Vernon J. Biever)*

Under coach Mike Holmgren, the Packers were like a family again. Brett and two teammates embrace after scoring another TD in 1997. *(Vernon J. Biever)*

Before the 1996 season even began, Brett experienced a major highlight: in July, he married longtime sweetheart Deanna Tynes. Favre then celebrated by leading the Packers to their first Super Bowl season in three decades.

(Vernon J. Biever)

Despite the menacing stare from a Buffalo defender, Brett has already done his job by plunging into the end zone for a touchdown.

(Vernon J. Biever)

Why is this man smiling? Maybe it's because it's another frigid day in Green Bay and Brett has never lost a single game in ice-cold weather. (Vernon J. Biever)

A relaxed Brett gives the thumbs-up sign as he prepares for his flight to Super Bowl XXXI. His confidence carried over to the field as he led the Packers to a championship victory over the New England Patriots. *(Vernon J. Biever)*

After winning the Super Bowl, the Packers visited the White House. Packers president Bob Harlan is at the microphone, flanked by President Bill Clinton and Brett Favre. *(Vernon J. Biever)*

Brett is sometimes at his best on a broken play. Here he scrambles out of the pocket just before completing a pass in Super Bowl XXXI. *(Vernon J. Biever)*

Brett's classic passing motion was on display against the
Denver Broncos in Super Bowl XXXII. Despite a fine game
by Brett, the Packers lost. *(Vernon J. Biever)*

liaison between Brett and Coach Holmgren. There were two young quarterbacks—Ty Detmer and Mark Brunell—raring to get some game action, just as Brett had been when Don Majkowski had his job. But even before the season began, Coach Holmgren made something perfectly clear to Brett. "I will not hesitate to pull you if we're losing games with the same mistakes we made last year," he said.

So Brett went out on the field with more pressure than ever before. He was told he had to perform and do it the coach's way. For the first month and a half of the season, Brett and the Packers were on something of a roller-coaster ride. They won their opener against Minnesota as Brett played it conservatively, going for the short and medium routes. He completed 22 of 36 passes for 185 yards and a touchdown. He didn't throw an intercept. The roller coaster was going up.

During the next two weeks, however, the Pack lost to Miami and Philadelphia. Brett had some big numbers, hitting 31 of 51 for 362 yards against Miami and 24 for 45 for 280 yards at Philly. But his 3 TD passes were matched by 3 intercepts, and the team lost both games. The roller coaster was headed downward.

A 30–3 victory over Tampa Bay followed as Brett connected on 30 of 39 for 306 yards and 3 scores. The coaster was climbing again. But a week later it plummeted in New England as Brett tossed a pair of intercepts and the Packers lost to the Patriots. A victory over the Rams sent the roller coaster back up, but a loss to the Vikings saw it heading down.

In the Viking game Brett threw an early interception, then had to leave the game at the end of the first quarter with a bruised hip.

Mark Brunell came on and played well, with the Vikings finally winning in overtime, 13–10. After seven games, the Packers were 3–4 and struggling. Brett had posted some big numbers but had thrown just 9 TD tosses and almost matched those with 7 pickoffs. Once again he was in Coach Holmgren's doghouse, and this time the clash between the two really came to a head. The coach was even thinking of installing the lefty-throwing Brunell at QB.

The coach pointed out that since getting the starting nod, Brett had thrown nearly as many interceptions (44) as touchdown passes (46). This was a totally unacceptable ratio. Holmgren's anger was apparent even when he spoke of Brett with a longtime friend, Bob LaMonte.

"I know Mike was livid with Brett," LaMonte said. "Mike told me at the time that it was just galling to see a player of this magnitude continue to self-destruct."

Quarterback coach Steve Mariucci called the days following the Minnesota game "the lowest point of [Brett's] Packers career." He said Brett threw a tantrum in his office because of his frustration over trying to master the team's complex offense. Brett's father was quite upset over what was transpiring with the Packers and his son. "I know my son," he said. "If Mike doesn't stop butchering him after he makes a mistake, Brett will dwindle to nothing."

At the regular coaches' meeting that week, Holmgren took a poll of the members of the offensive staff, asking which quarterback they felt should be the starter, Brett or understudy Mark Brunell. It was later reported that Brunell actually won the vote. The coaches felt at that time that he was a better decision-maker than Brett. But the final call would have to come from Mike Holmgren.

The coach thought about it, taking into consideration his history with Brett, the opinions of his coaches, and his own desire to get into the Super Bowl. When he called Brett into his office, many felt he would tell his quarterback that there would be a change. But the coach fooled everyone.

"Buddy, it's your job," he told Brett. Then he added, "We're joined at the hip now. Either we're going to the Super Bowl together, or we're going down together."

That was it. No more quarterback controversy. Coach Holmgren apparently had made his decision from a gut feeling that, despite everything, Brett Favre was still the man who could bring the team back to the glory of the Lombardi years. He also felt that Brett was close to mastering the offense and that his only remaining fault—his tendency to freelance and force situations—was something they could correct.

Brett would later admit that his own personality was partly responsible for the tension between player and coach.

"I probably drove Mike crazy more than once," he said. "I've always been the kind of guy who questions authority. I did it with my dad when he was coaching me in high school. A lot of the things he told me went in one ear and out the other."

Of course when Brett heard he was not going to be replaced by Mark Brunell, who eventually moved on and became a star in his own right with the Jacksonville Jaguars, he was happy. But he still had reservations about the offense, which he voiced to Steve Mariucci.

"I told Brett, 'You've got two choices,'" Maruiucci said. "'You can go in the tank and feel sorry for yourself. Or you can buckle down, shake it off, and be the best quarterback in football [for] the rest of the season.' Know what he told me? He said, 'The second half of the season is going to be like no other.'"

Chapter 8

Becoming the MVP

Brett started the next game at Chicago in horrible conditions. It was cold and windy, with a hard, driving rain falling throughout the entire game. Not the kind of day to throw the football. With the ball on the Chicago 36 in the second period, Brett rolled out, tucked the ball in, and ran downfield. He dived over the final Chicago defender at the goal line for a score.

In the fourth period he drove the Pack downfield again and this time connected with Edgar Bennett on a 13-yard touchdown strike, raising the Packers' lead to 27–0. His final stats showed him completing just 6 of 15 passes for 82 yards. But he also ran for 58 yards and led his team to an easy win under trying conditions. It was later called one of his finest performances of the year.

Next the Pack hosted the Detroit Lions, and this

time the weather was good and Brett looked great. He completed 24 of 36 passes for 237 yards and 3 touchdowns. Although he was picked off once, it didn't affect the outcome. The Packers won again.

A week later Brett was 20 of 28, a 71.4 completion percentage, with 2 scores and no intercepts as the Pack took the New York Jets, 17–10, for the team's third straight victory. But after that, the ball club faltered and dropped three in a row. It was actually a defensive letdown, however, as Brett continued to perform brilliantly.

The Packers' losses were all on the road—to Buffalo, Dallas, and Detroit. Although the team came up short, Brett threw for 214, 257, and 366 yards in the trio of contests. He also connected for 10 touchdown passes against just 3 interceptions. But the three defeats could have been a deathblow to the season. They left the club with a 6–7 mark and made them a long shot to reach the playoffs. To have a chance, they would absolutely have to win their remaining three games.

First they easily whipped the Bears, 40–3, as Brett threw for three more scores. That victory enabled the Pack to even its record at 7–7. Next came a must-win game with Atlanta. Brett always wanted to play well against the Falcons, the team that had given up on him back in 1991. That contest, though, wasn't nearly as easy as the game with the Bears had been. The Falcons played tough and took a 17–14 lead going into the final period. Once again Brett would have to lead his team from behind.

As had happened so often, the game came down

to the final minutes. The Packers still trailed by 3 points as they got the ball at their own 33-yard line. They were 67 yards from the end zone with just 1:58 remaining on the clock. Brett really had his work cut out for him. Using Coach Holmgren's controlled-passing game, Brett worked the team downfield without benefit of a running play. He completed 6 of 9 passes in the drive and brought the ball to the 9-yard line with less than 20 seconds left. A field goal would tie it, but the Green Bay fans on sidelines wanted the win.

When Brett called signals, the Falcons' defense expected him to throw. But this time he took off around the right side and dived into the corner of the end zone for the winning touchdown with just 14 seconds left on the clock. The extra point gave the Packers a 21–14 victory and kept their playoff hopes alive. For the game, Brett completed 29 of 44 passes for 321 yards and 2 scores. If he wanted to show the Falcons they had made a big mistake by letting him get away, he had succeeded.

The Pack still one more game to win. This one was at Tampa Bay, a Battle of the Bays, as people liked to call the Green Bay–Tampa Bay games. As the Buccaneers found out, Brett and the Packers were not about to be stopped. Brett cranked up his strong right arm to the tune of 24 of 36 passes for 291 yards and 3 scores, all of them going to Sterling Sharpe. Green Bay won the game big, 34–19, to finish at 9–7 for a third straight year. Fortunately it was good enough to get them into the playoffs as a wild-card entry.

The victory, however, would prove very costly.

After catching three scoring passes from Brett, receiver Sterling Sharpe injured his neck late in the game. Subsequent examination revealed a serious injury that would require surgery. After the operation, Sharpe was told it would be too risky for him to resume his playing career, and he was forced to retire. Not only had Sharpe been a record setter, but he was Brett's favorite target and one of the best wideouts of his generation. His premature retirement was a loss for everyone.

In his final season, Sharpe still had great numbers. He had caught 94 passes for 1,119 yards with 18 of them going for touchdowns. That was the most TDs among all the receivers in the NFL. Now the Packers would have to go into the playoffs without him.

Brett, too, had put together a great season. His final numbers were 363 completions in 582 attempts, good for a 62.4 percentage. He wound up throwing 33 touchdown passes with just 14 interceptions for a final quarterback efficiency rating of 90.7, best of his career to date. Only league MVP Steve Young of the 49ers had a higher rating. Brett's 33 scoring passes were second to Young's 35 and set a new Packers record.

More interesting, however, was the change in Brett after the midseason crisis that almost saw him benched. From the time Coach Holmgren gave him a vote of confidence and Brett told Steve Mariucci that the rest of the year would be like no other, Brett soared. In the final nine games of the year, he threw for 24 touchdowns and had just 7 passes intercepted. That was one reason he was named second-team All-Pro by *Football Digest* magazine.

Coach Holmgren was very pleased with the way Brett played in the final nine games of year. Those performances convinced him that he had made the right decision by committing to Brett. In fact, he compared Brett with Steve Young, the only quarterback who had a better year than Brett did in 1994. Holmgren, while an assistant coach at San Francisco, had worked with Young.

"[Steve] and Brett are so much alike in a lot of ways," the coach said. "Both are fierce battlers, and Steve is every bit as hardheaded as Brett. He thinks he knows more about it than you do. He's a tough case, which is the mark of a lot of great ones. They want to win so badly, they set incredible expectations for themselves, and they can be hard on everybody.

"But I wanted Brett to understand that while he could do some amazing things, inventing plays on the fly, we still wanted him to stick with the system, learn it as completely as he could, and take all the easy stuff first. Only then should he look for Plan B and throw the ball away if he had to. Brett would rather go to the dentist than just give up on a play and throw the ball out-of-bounds."

Obviously, coach and quarterback were closer than before. Holmgren was too smart to harness Brett completely. As long as he played within the system most of the time, the coach was happy. And face it, he didn't want to take away Brett's ability to make the big play when it didn't appear to be there. That was a talent very few signal callers had.

The playoffs following the 1994 season were a repeat of those from the previous year. In the wild-card game, the Packers again played the Detroit Lions. Only this time the Lions were also a wild-card team. The two met at Lambeau Field on December 31. The temperature was a brisk 33 degrees. Brett still had not quarterbacked a losing game when the temperature was below 35.

This one was no different—but it was close. Brett had to play ball-control football. Without Sharpe in the lineup, he stayed with short- and medium-range throws, taking time off the clock and directing several long drives. When it ended, Brett had completed 23 of 38 passes for 262 yards. He didn't throw a touchdown pass, but he wasn't picked off, either. His ball-control passing game resulted in a 16–12 Green Bay victory.

Now the Packers would have to meet the Dallas Cowboys, the defending Super Bowl champions. This was the one team they couldn't seem to beat. And once again the Cowboys were just too strong. They handed the Packers an embarassing 35–9 defeat, containing the Green Bay passing game as Brett hit on just 18 of 35 for 211 yards. He was intercepted once and failed to throw a touchdown pass. It was not an ideal way to end a season.

Brett and the Pack had been 9–7 for three straight years now. Ironically, Coach Holmgren had told Brett earlier that if he didn't improve he would always be a 9–7 quarterback. But after the vote of confidence midway through the season, Brett had led the club to a 6–3 mark. The 1995 season would be the fourth year with Mike Holmgren at the helm and Brett Favre as the quarter-back. This time around, a 9–7 record would not be acceptable.

There were questions after the opening game, in which the team lost to a St. Louis Rams ball club that was not considered on a par with the Packers. Brett had to play from behind all afternoon, hitting 29 of 51 passes for 299 yards and a pair of scores. But he was intercepted three times and some fans wondered which Brett Favre they would see—the one who had played the first seven games the season before or the All-Pro who had led the team in the last nine.

A week later, however, Brett really gave his fans a preview of things to come. The Packers were playing at Chicago, and Brett looked strong and confident from the start. In the second quarter a Chicago punt drove the Packers back to their own one-yard line. Brett came out, huddled up, then stepped to the line. He dropped back into the end zone, looked downfield, and saw that he had good protection, so he fired the ball high and deep downfield.

The pass was perfect. Wide receiver Robert Brooks, who was behind his defender, caught the ball in midstride and raced all the way to the end zone to complete a spectacular 99-yard touchdown play. It was only the eighth time in NFL history that a touchdown pass of that length had been completed. Brett went on to throw for 312 yards and 3 TDs as the Packers got their first win of the season.

They would go on to win four of the next five, with Brett beginning to rack up big, big numbers.

He threw for 342 yards against Detroit with a pair of scores, then followed it with a 295-yard effort and 4 touchdown passes in a 38–21 win over Minnesota. For his efforts in that game, Brett was named NFC Offensive Player of the Week. Then, however, a pair of off games followed, losses to Detroit and Minnesota in which Brett threw just a single touchdown and was intercepted five times.

Late in the second quarter of the Minnesota game, Brett was hit hard by several Vikings and got up slowly. He was limping on his left ankle and had to leave the game. Backup Ty Detmer came on to finish the half. Brett tried three series in the third quarter, but the ankle was hindering him too much. He had to leave again, and the team lost. Suddenly the Packers were just 5–4 and with their top quarterback injured. It had all the earmarks of another 9–7 season. Those familiar with the recent history of the Pack waited for another Holmgren-Favre explosion.

It didn't happen. As the coach had said the year before, the two were joined at the hip. Holmgren knew that Brett was his quarterback, the one most capable of helping the team to the Super Bowl. His biggest concern was getting Brett healthy enough to start against the Bears the following week. But the ankle was just the latest in a string of minor injuries.

Brett had had surgery the previous January to repair a herniated muscle in his right side. At the time doctors told him it might take a full year for the muscle to heal normally. Brett started a preseason game less than eight months later. After the first seven games of the 1995 season, Brett was already suffering from a throbbing turf toe, a bruised right shoulder, an arthritic right hip, a bruised left knee, and a sore lower back. Then in week nine, he sustained the badly sprained ankle.

Playing in pain had been a Favre trademark since his days at Southern Mississippi. In fact, backup QB Ty Detmer once said, "Brett's not coming out of a game unless a bone is sticking out."

Like many players in the NFL, Brett began taking medication to help him deal with the minor injuries and pain. In his case, he began using a prescription painkiller called Vicodin, described as a narcotic analgesic. The Vicodin was one reason he could play on, but its full effect wouldn't be known until after the season. In the meantime, a week after suffering the severe ankle injury against Minnesota, Brett returned to the starting lineup to face the Bears.

There was no evidence of the bad ankle. Brett simply shredded the Bears' defense by hitting 75.8 percent of his passes (25 of 33) for 336 yards and 5 touchdowns. He wasn't picked off even once, and the Packers needed every one of his scoring aerials as they won, 35–28. That game marked the beginning of the hottest streak of Brett's career, and perhaps marked the change from his being a fine quarterback to being a bona fide superstar.

Starting with the Bears game on November 12, Brett and the Packers would win six of their final seven contests. And in those games Brett arguably played as well as any quarterback who ever lived.

His numbers were awesome. It was as if Brett were playing on another level.

At Cleveland he completed 82.1 percent of his passes with 3 touchdowns. He threw for 3 more against Tampa Bay and another 3 in a 24–10 victory over Cincinnati, a game in which he passed for 339 yards. Two weeks after that he fired 4 scoring passes in a 34–23 victory over New Orleans that clinched the NFC Central Division title for the Pack. Then, a week later, he closed out the regular season by throwing for 301 yards and 2 scores in a 24–10 victory over the always tough Pittsburgh Steelers.

In the seven games following his ankle injury at Minnesota, Brett hit on 166 of 236 passes for a 70.3 completion percentage. In that span, he threw for 2,046 yards and had an amazing 21 touchdown passes against just 2 interceptions. His quarterback efficiency rating for those games was an incredible 123.0. Suddenly the mistakes of past years weren't there. He was so good that he was named NFC Offensive Player of the Month for December.

The Packers were division champs with an 11–5 record. They had finally broken the three-year run of 9–7 seasons. Brett Favre had become the quarterback many people had predicted he could be. For the season he completed 359 of 570 passes for a league-leading 4,413 yards. His completion percentage stood at 63.0, and he threw for an NFC record 38 touchdowns—the third-highest total in league history—and he had just 13 passes picked off. His quarterback efficiency rating for the year was an NFC-best 99.5.

Shortly afterward, the honors began to come. They were almost too numerous to mention. He was selected to start for the NFC in the postseason Pro Bowl. The *Sporting News, Football Digest,* Miller Lite, the Maxwell Club, and the Touchdown Club of Columbus all named him their NFL Player of the Year. He earned a slew of Offensive Player of the Year awards and was a first-team All-Pro selection of the Associated Press and United Press International. The Professional Football Writers of America, *Pro Football Weekly,* and *Sports Illustrated* all named him the league's Most Valuable Player.

And in the official vote, the Associated Press named him the NFL's Most Valuable Player for 1995. He had come full circle.

Chapter 9

The Playoffs and a Major Crisis

Awards and individual honors are great. A player can take great pride in these accomplishments, and they can certainly help him to earn more money come contract time. But if you asked any professional athlete, nearly every one would trade individual awards for a team championship. Like that of his teammates, Brett's ultimate goal was to win the Super Bowl.

The Green Bay offense had thrived in 1995 despite the loss of Sterling Sharpe. Robert Brooks had emerged as an All-Pro receiver, catching 102 passes for 1,497 yards and 13 touchdowns. Running back Edgar Bennett had cracked the 1,000-yard barrier for the first time in his career. And tight end Mark Chmura was also becoming an outstanding player, teaming with veteran All-Pro Keith Jackson to give defenses double trouble while adding another dimension to Brett's passing game. Defensively the team wasn't quite up to the offense. They still gave up too many points, but they were becoming more balanced, with talented players manning a number of key positions.

In the first round of the playoffs, the Pack played host to Brett's old team, the Atlanta Falcons. The 9–7 Falcons had made the playoffs as a wild card. Green Bay, of course, was the heavy favorite. The game was played in 30-degree weather, with a light fog enveloping Lambeau Field. Before the game, someone pointed out that Brett had a 13–0 cold-weather record since taking over as the Packers' quarterback.

The team's detractors continued to point to the Pack's soft regular-season schedule, in which they faced just four playoff teams all year. The team had also lost two individual stars following the 1994 season—wide receiver Sharpe to injury and defensive lineman Bryce Paup to free agency. But Coach Holmgren felt those losses had helped the team come together.

"Because we had lost a couple of star players— and I mean legitimate star players—I felt the team concept of football would really be tested this year," the coach said. "I felt good about that, but trying to convince other people was a chore sometimes."

Brett didn't need convincing. Always supremely confident, he was just one of the Packers who felt the team should be considered a real threat in the playoffs.

"We feel we can go all the way," Brett said. "One

step is down [winning the division], and we have another one to go [the playoffs]. We can play better, and we have to in every phase, if we want to keep playing."

The Falcons wouldn't be easy to beat because of their offense. They used the run-and-shoot, triggered by quarterback Jeff George, who was sometimes erratic but was capable of brilliance. With three 1,000-yard receivers and a 1,000-yard rusher supporting him, George was capable of putting a lot of points on the board. The game was expected to be a real shoot-out.

George wasted no time in showing the Packers how the run-and-shoot worked. Just three minutes into the game, the strong-armed Falcons QB rifled a 65-yard touchdown pass to speedy wide receiver Eric Metcalf. The extra point made it a 7–0 game. So right away, Brett and his teammates were playing from behind. In the past that might have thrown them off their game, but not this time.

Following a 42-yard kickoff return by rookie Antonio Freeman, Brett drove the Packers down to the Atlanta eight, where Edgar Bennett carried the ball in for the score. The extra point tied it at 7–7. Minutes later, Brett led the Pack on a 78-yard drive and culminated it with a 14-yard TD toss to Robert Brooks. The kick made it 14–7, and the Pack had the lead. From that point, Brett and the offense just picked the Falcons apart.

George made one more big play, hitting wideout Terrance Mathis with a 55-yard bomb to set up a Morten Andersen field goal that cut the lead to 14–10. But the Pack came right back when Antonio

Freeman returned a punt 76 yards for yet another Packers' score. The point was missed, but the lead was now 20–10, and it wasn't even halftime. Then in the closing minutes of the second period, Brett drove the Packers 85 yards with a perfect time-consuming ball-control march. He finished it with a 2-yard touchdown toss to tight end Mark Chmura. The kick made it 27–10 at halftime— Green Bay in command.

Brett had been brilliant in the first two sessions. He threw to nine different receivers and completed 16 of 22 passes for 115 yards. Two other passes were on the mark but were dropped. He had played an almost perfect half of football. The third period was scoreless until Atlanta got a touchdown early in the fourth to make it 27–17. With the lead back to 10 points, Brett got his club on the board again.

This time he drove them 70 yards, once again eating up the clock, and finished the drive with an 18-yard pass to rookie running back Dorsey Levens. The kick made it 34–17. Before it ended, both clubs traded field goals, bringing the final score to 37–20. The Pack had won it and were moving on to the divisional playoff game for the third straight year.

Brett finished the game against the Falcons with 24 completions in 35 attempts for 199 yards, 3 touchdowns, and no interceptions. Bennett carried the ball 24 times for a Packer playoff record 108 yards as the balanced attack did in the Falcons. After the game Brett said he felt the team had proved something and was now a worthy contender to defeat the San Francisco 49ers, their next opponents.

"You don't have to throw for 400 yards to be successful," he said. "I threw three touchdowns today, and we were precise when we had to be. If [the 49ers] were watching today, they know not to take us lightly."

The Niners were defending Super Bowl champs and had compiled an 11–5 record during the season. Their offense was led by superstar quarterback Steve Young and superstar wide receiver Jerry Rice. In addition, their defense was considered superior to that of the Packers. But the Packers were a poised and confident group.

"This is the most unselfish group I've ever been around as a coach," Mike Holmgren said.

Rookie receiver Antonio Freeman seconded that thought. "The unity on this team is extraordinary," he said. "I've never experienced anything like it in my life. It's like your teammates are your biggest fans. You can't ask for much more than that."

Critics, however, pointed to the fact that the team was relying too much on the talents of Brett Favre. There was a feeling in the clubhouse that if the game was close, Brett was the guy who would find a way to get the job done, to win it. In fact, when safety Leroy Butler was asked for three reasons why he believed the Packers would win he answered without hesitation. "Brett, Brett, Brett" was all he said.

Like all the great ones, Brett was always willing to bear the burden of being the main man. When told of Butler's remarks, he answered, "That's great. To me as a player that's what you want them to say, that we're putting it all on Brett."

But Brett also knew that the team need a solid game from his defense. "I want Leroy [Butler] to know we need a little help out of [the defense], too. We're going to put up as many points as we can. If they can hold them, you know, we can win this ball game."

The game was played on January 6 at Candlestick Park in San Francisco. Before the game, some of the 49ers were watching Brett warm up. His passes seemed to be fluttering, not sharp, and many of the veteran Niners thought the twenty-six-year-old MVP was nervous.

"Why be nervous?" Brett said when asked about pregame jitters. "If we lose, everyone expects it. If we win, we're kings. We came to play."

That turned out to be an understatement. Brett came out and quickly showed the Niner defense he wasn't nervous—not a bit nervous, in fact. On the Packers' first possession of the day, Brett engineered a near-perfect seven-minute 48-yard drive. Though it ended with a blocked field goal, it set the tone for the rest of the game.

The first score came with a little more than seven minutes left in the quarter, when Steve Young threw a quick pass to fullback Adam Walker. Green Bay linebacker Wayne Simmons hit Walker like a truck, jarring the ball loose. Rookie cornerback Craig Newsome scooped up the fumble and ran it 31 yards to the end zone for a score. The kick gave the Pack a 7–0 lead. Then, some three minutes later, Brett drove the Packers downfield again and hit Keith Jackson with a 2-yard scoring pass. Add Chris Jacke's extra point and the score was 14–0.

Early in the second period the Packers were driving again. This time Brett dropped back and rifled a bullet to Mark Chmura from 13 yards out. Jacke's point made it a 21–0 game, the Packers in command. A late Niner field goal made it 21–3 at the half. Anyone looking at the halftime numbers could see clearly that the dominant player on the field had been Brett Favre.

Brett completed 15 of his first 16 passes and, by intermission, had hit on 15 of 17 for 222 yards and 2 scores. He was close to unstoppable. From there the Packers cruised to a 27–17 victory. Although the Niners came within 10 points, the outcome was never in doubt. In fact, it was 27–10 when the Niners scored their final touchdown with less than a minute left.

When it was over, Brett had completed 21 of 28 passes for 299 yards in a brilliant performance, maybe his best of the year. Brooks caught 4 passes for 103 yards, while Jackson grabbed 4 for 101. So Brett made them all count. But there was more ahead. Now the Pack was in the NFC championship game. The problem was that they would have to play their longtime nemesis, the Dallas Cowboys.

It was the Cowboys who had come closest to stopping Lombardi's Packer teams in the 1960s. Back then the Pack always prevailed. The 1990s Cowboys were a powerhouse, having won two straight Super Bowls after the 1992 and 1993 seasons. The Niners dethroned them a year earlier, but once again Dallas was the favorite to go all the way. In addition, they had won five straight over the Pack, including regular-season and playoff games in 1993 and 1994, and a regular-season game on October 8, when the Cowboys emerged with a 34–24 victory.

But the Packers were confident they could win this time. Brett was being touted as the hottest player in the playoffs. In two games he had completed 45 of 63 passes (71 percent) for 498 yards, 5 touchdowns, and no interceptions. His quarterback rating was 121.0.

"Brett Favre is playing so well that the Packers can beat anybody, any time, anywhere," said safety Leroy Butler. "We feel that if you can go into the playoffs being real hot, you can overcome a lot of adversity. And we're on a roll right now."

Coach Holmgren said his players were on a mission. "We're *not* just glad to be here," said the coach, referring to the championship game. "The win against San Francisco was the biggest win we've had here, and the players were euphoric for about an hour. All of a sudden, on the airplane, they realized we still have some unfinished business."

Brett, for one, said emphatically that his team was ready. "[Against the 49ers] we just wanted to make a statement that we were one of the elite teams in this league," he said. "[As for Dallas], each time we went down there [in the past] we didn't feel we belonged in that building with them. Now we do."

Beating the Cowboys and winning the Super Bowl was the Pack's obvious goal. It was Brett's goal as well. Since the quarterback is usually the focal point of a championship team, winning the Super Bowl is always considered the final touch of greatness. It may not be fair, but that's the way it is. Even Coach Holmgren acknowledged that fact when he spoke about Dallas quarterback Troy Aikman and Brett.

"Troy has obviously taken his team to the Super Bowl, which is the measuring stick for all great quarterbacks," Holmgren said. "You can have great stats and throw the ball for 4,000 yards, but the true measuring stick for quarterbacks in this league is Super Bowl wins. Troy has done that. Brett hasn't done that yet."

Brett said he was relaxed before the title tilt, adding, "It's just a game. If I ever knew how many people were counting on what I did, I'd go nuts."

Finally it was time for that next step. The two teams met on January 14, 1996, at Texas Stadium. Brett came out pumped up—something that would often become a trademark in big games. He was too pumped, too strong, and his first three passes were high and wild.

"I came in fairly relaxed," Brett would say. "Right before the game I got fairly excited."

Green Bay actually scored first on a 46-yard field goal. But the Cowboys bounced back to score a pair of touchdowns, both on Aikman to Michael Irvin passes. The second drive started after defensive lineman Leon Lett picked off one of Brett's throws. At that point, Brett was 0-for-6 with one interception. With just 2:20 left in the first quarter, the Cowboys already had a 14–3 lead.

The Packers ran the kickoff back to their own 27, and Brett came out on the field once more. On the very first play he dropped back and looked downfield for Robert Brooks. Then he let it fly, a perfect strike to the streaking Brooks, who caught it in midstride and completed the 73-yard touchdown play. Brett's first completion of the day had closed the Dallas lead to 14–10. And he had answered the second Cowboy score in just 21 seconds.

After that the game became a real dogfight. Brett struck again just 39 seconds into the second quarter. This time he hit Keith Jackson from 24 yards out for another score. Jacke's extra point gave the Pack a 17–14 lead. Brett seemed to be back on his game, and the Packers had already shown they were ready to give the Cowboys a battle.

Dallas was a veteran team—its big stars were too poised to roll over. They tied the game on a field goal midway through the period, then reclaimed the lead when Emmitt Smith ran the ball in from the 1-yard line just seconds before the half. So at intermission the Cowboys had a 24–17 lead. But after intermission it was the Packers' turn. A 37-yard Jacke field goal and a 1-yard TD toss from Brett to Robert Brooks gave Green Bay a 27–24 lead after three. The Packers were now just 15 minutes away from a possible trip to the Super Bowl.

But the Cowboys had been wearing the Packer defense down with power runs by Emmitt Smith behind their great offensive line. At the outset of the fourth quarter, Aikman and Smith led the Cowboys as they completed an 8-minute, 90-yard drive that had begun toward the end of the third period. Smith finally scored from the 5, and Dallas had regained the lead, 31–27. More than 12 minutes still remained for Brett to work his magic.

Green Bay began driving from its own 22-yard line. Helped by an 18-yard run by Edgar Bennett, Brett moved the team to the Dallas 46. On first down he dropped back again, looking downfield for wide receiver Mark Ingram, who was flying down the right sideline. Brett expected Ingram to come back on the ball, and that's how he threw it. But Ingram kept going, and Dallas cornerback Larry Brown had an easy interception, bringing the ball back to his own 48.

From there it took the Cowboys just two plays to put the game on ice. First Aikman hit Irvin for a 36-yard gain to the Green Bay 16. And on the next play, Emmitt Smith ran it right up the gut and into the end zone. The kick made it 38–27, and that's the way it ended. The Cowboys returned to the Super Bowl and won it for the third time in four years. The Packers would be going home a step wiser and a step closer. But not yet there.

Brett finished the game with 21 completions in 39 attempts for 307 yards. He had 3 TD passes and 2 picks. Troy Aikman was 21 of 33 for 255 yards with 2 TDs and no intercepts. Smith ran for 150 yards and 3 scores. He might have been the difference.

"[Brown's] interception was the turning point," Brett said. "The game was going back and forth. We wanted to hang in there and keep it close at the end and see what happens. We were four quarters away from the Super Bowl. This was a stepladder season for us. I'd like to think next year is the Super Bowl. I feel good about what we've done. Unfortunately it had to end this way. It's upsetting."

All told, Brett had put together a brilliant season, one of the best any quarterback had ever had. The team was still building, still developing, and its quarterback was just twenty-six years old.

As Coach Holmgren said, "[Brett] means everything to us. I can't say enough good things about the young man. The sky is the limit."

Once the sting of defeat abated, it should have been a great off-season for Brett. After all, he collected a slew of individual awards, was the league's Most Valuable Player, and was being called the next great quarterback in the game. Everyone wanted him. He was beginning to get more off-field endorsements, and he had a very big financial future.

His personal life should also have been very happy. He had been seeing the same girl, Deanna Tynes, since 1985. The couple had a daughter, Brittany, who was born on February 6, 1989. They were planning to get married in the near future.

Very few people outside the Packer family suspected that something might be wrong. The story didn't come out publicly until February 27. Brett was in Bellin Hospital in Green Bay, where he had just undergone surgery to remove a bone spur and several bone chips from his left ankle. That was the one he had hurt in the Minnesota game back on November 5.

Brett was talking to Deanna, their daughter, and a nurse when he suddenly went into an unexpected and violent seizure. The nurse called frantically for help. The doctors first made sure Brett didn't swallow his tongue; then they quickly hooked up a series of IVs and machines to see what had caused the seizure. When Brett asked what had happened, Dr. John Gray, the Packers' associate team physician said, "You've just suffered a seizure, Brett. People can die from those."

That's when Brett realized he might have a problem. He had been taking the painkilling drug Vicodin, for most of the season. For the first time he admitted that he had become dependent on the drug and that his heavy use of it might have contributed to the seizure. When the story finally broke, it made headlines. Here was perhaps the toughest quarterback in the NFL admitting he might have a dependence on the prescription drug that had just helped him produce a super season.

Pain, of course, is part of every football player's life. Brett's was no exception. Quarterbacks can take a fearsome pounding almost every week. They start playing in high school, then play through four years of college, and then move on to the pros, and that adds up to years of pounding and many hours of pain. In addition to playing every season, Brett had had five operations in six years, beginning with abdominal surgery following his car accident in 1990.

The public didn't know about Brett's problem until he held a press conference in Green Bay on May 14. At that time he announced that because he had developed a dependency on prescription pain-killers, he was entering the Menninger Clinic in Topeka, Kansas. It was a gutsy move on Brett's part. He allowed the story to come out and for a very specific reason.

"I'm sure there are a ton of NFL players out there who'll watch me come out and say to them-selves, 'Man, that's me.' That's one reason I'm talking," Brett said. "I hope I can help some players get help. I realize now how dangerous it is to keep using these things."

Brett had the longest streak of consecutive starts of any quarterback in the league—68 straight games through the 1995 season. The desire not to let his team down and the fear of losing his job to injury were the major reasons he fell into chemi-cal dependence.

"I'm not blaming anyone," he said. "It's my fault. The only reason I ever did this was because I had to. *Had* to. I had to play. Injuries have cost a lot of guys their jobs in this league, and there was no way an injury was ever going to cost me my job. Then it got out of hand."

As the injuries mounted during the season, Brett had begun using Vicodin very heavily. His use of it increased during the second half of the season.

Deanne Tynes was one of the first to realize something was wrong. "Brett would ask me to ask friends for Vicodin," she said. "But I wasn't about to do that."

As the season wore on, some of his closest Packer friends began to suspect that Brett was developing a serious problem. In addition to the doses the doctor prescribed, Brett was getting the painkiller from teammates who didn't finish their prescriptions and then from doctors outside the Packer organization.

"I started finding pills everywhere," Deanna Tynes said. "I'd catch him throwing up badly. Some nights he wouldn't sleep, just sit in front of the TV for hours or play solitaire on the computer. I'd ask him what was wrong, reminding him that he had meetings at eight in the morning and still hadn't been to bed."

Yet Brett continued to play outstanding football. He also worked out like a demon with the team's strength coach.

Teammate and friend Mark Chmura said, "We'd tell him time and again, 'You've got to cut this out.' But players think they're invincible, and Brett was no different. He'd be fine for the games because I think he didn't do much of it on the weekend. But some weekday nights he'd be zapped."

Deanna Tynes said she demanded that Brett stop taking Vicodin when he was at the Pro Bowl in Hawaii in early February. He said he would stop, but he didn't. Then, at the ESPN-sponsored ESPY Awards in New York on February 12, Tynes noticed that Brett was slurring his words more and more as the night went on, but he wasn't drinking. Later she asked him what he had been taking. He said he'd taken a couple of Vicodins. When she pressed even harder, he admitted he had taken some thirteen pills. But it was only after his seizure in the hospital that Brett knew he had to confront his problem.

He stopped taking the pills immediately. Then he began attending sessions with NFL-assigned counselors in Chicago and New Orleans. The whole ordeal was an emotional roller coaster for Brett. At one point, he told Deanna, "I may be a successful football player, but I feel like such a failure. How could I let this happen?"

Finally, in May, Brett held his press conference to announce that he was going to the Menninger Clinic.

"I quit taking Vicodin cold turkey after my seizure," he said, "and I entered the rehab center because I want to make sure I'm totally clean. The counselors I've seen think it's best for me. The one thing they've taught me is that there will always be a spot in your brain that wants it."

The one thing that bothered Brett was that he would be perceived as a "druggie." Because he was in an NFL-sanctioned program, he was also prohibited from drinking alcohol, which he said was not part of his problem. But the program called for him to stop drinking for two years. He would be tested randomly and could be suspended for four games if any test for alcohol came back positive.

As with everything else he had done in life, Brett tackled his stay at Menninger with an upbeat attitude and a desire to turn it into something positive. He worked out and did more running than he ever had. His weight dropped from 230 to 218 pounds, and his body fat was down from 18 percent to just 8 percent. When he emerged from the clinic after 45 days, he was in the best physical condition of his life. But there was something he wanted to make very clear: while admitting he had to deal with a very serious problem, Brett wanted to emphasize that his case was different from that of someone who decides to take drugs on his own. He didn't want people to equate him with some-one who voluntarily begins using so-called recreational drugs like marijuana and cocaine. His dependency came from a medication that doctors had prescribed to help him deal with pain. From now on, he would take only over-the-counter pain medications, the same ones the average person uses for headaches or arthritis.

When he emerged, all those who knew and loved Brett were overjoyed. His teammates wel-comed him, and his longtime love, Deanna Tynes, said, "I can't believe it. The old Brett's back."

Brett sounded a warning to all those who think they are on top of the world and will stay there, no matter what. Something he said when he entered the Menninger deserves to be repeated over and over: "I'm twenty-six years old. I just threw thirty-eight touchdown passes in one year, and I'm the NFL MVP. People look at me and say, 'I'd love to be that guy.' But if they knew what it took to be that guy, they wouldn't love to be him, I can guarantee you that. I'm entering a treatment center tomorrow. Would they love that?"

Chapter 10

Super at Last

It was a turbulent off-season for Brett in more ways than one. His dependence on Vicodin and subsequent rehabilitation grabbed the lion's share of the headlines. In early July he called Packers general manager Ron Wolf to let him know he was ready to play. "Don't worry," Brett told the GM. "We're going to the Super Bowl. And I really believe that. We're a better team."

Then he spoke about his personal incentives: "I've got so much driving me. Number one, I won the MVP award last year, and that thrill lasted about a week and a half. We lost to the Cowboys in the NFC championship game, and it was like the MVP didn't matter. Two, the [Super Bowl] is in New Orleans, right near my home. Three, I want to prove everyone wrong who thinks I'm some drug addict. Four, I want to do it for Reggie

[White]. I tell every guy every day: we're only playing for one thing."

He also sounded a warning to those who might feel his game would suffer because of his dependency and rehab. "I have one thing to say to all the people expecting me to fail: go ahead, bet against me," he said.

Then, in mid-July, there was a happy event. Brett and longtime sweetheart Deanna Tynes were married. They had been a family with daughter Brittany for years. Now the status of their relationship was official. Even Deanna sounded a warning to those doubting her husband. "Brett doesn't want Vicodin anymore," she said. "He wants just one thing—the Super Bowl."

But if his marriage to Deanna was a high point, there was a low point shortly afterward. His older brother, Scott, was driving a car that was struck by a train. A passenger in the vehicle, one of Brett's closest friends, was killed. When the investigation was complete, Scott was charged with felony drunk driving. It was a dual tragedy that everyone in the Favre family had to endure.

So Brett came to training camp with a heavy heart, a sense of having something to prove to everyone, and a bit of a chip on his shoulder. Coach Holmgren said the reason was that many people had the wrong perception, that they felt Brett's success had something to do with drugs. "People think last year he was in dreamland half the time," the coach said, "and that was not the way it was."

Brett was even more specific. One reporter

asked him what it was like to take a Vicodin during a game. That angered Brett, since he had never taken the medication during games or on Fridays or Saturdays, the days preceding the games.

Finally he popped off. "It's kind of like when I threw twenty-four interceptions [in 1993]," Brett explained, "and people said, 'I knew the Packers made a mistake getting him [from Atlanta the year before].' Then I come back the next year, and they go, 'Well, he's got good talent around him now.' And now they're saying, 'No wonder he played well last year. He was taking pills.' There's never been a time in my life when people just said, 'You know what? He's just pretty damn good.'"

Those excuses may have been the perception of just a few, but they were one of the ways Brett was motivating himself for the 1996 season. He also found a way to work around the pain he knew would come again from being an NFL quarterback. This time Vicodin would not play a role—that was in the past. Instead, if he felt he needed something, he simply relied on over-the-counter products such as anti-inflammatory medications. He also found that regular exercise helped him both physically and mentally.

"If I take a day off [from exercising], the pain comes back," he said, explaining that he was working to maintain the level of conditioning he had attained at the Menninger Clinic. He often did wind sprints on a treadmill the day before a game and again right after the game. So when the 1996 season got under way, both Brett and the Packers were ready.

The team had been adding better players. For instance, the defensive line now consisted of Reggie White and Sean Jones at the ends, Gilbert Brown and Santana Dotson at tackle. That was an outstanding front four. Safety Eugene Robinson came over from Seattle to team with Leroy Butler, giving the Pack two of the better safeties in the league.

Robert Brooks and speedy Antonio Freeman were at wide receiver, compensating for the loss of Sterling Sharpe the year before. Veteran Don Beebe, who had been to the Super Bowl with the Buffalo Bills, gave the young players a steadying presence. Flashy Desmond Howard, a former Heisman Trophy winner, signed on as a free agent. He was another wide receiver and a dangerous kickoff and punt returner. Keith Jackson and Mark Chmura were as talented a pair of tight ends as any duo in the league.

Edgar Bennett and the improving Dorsey Levens gave the team two solid running backs, both of whom could catch the ball out of the backfield. Fullback William Henderson was a rock. The offensive line was very solid. And then there was Brett. He and Reggie White were considered the heart and soul of the team. When Brett had said he wanted a Super Bowl win for Reggie, he knew how long the defensive end had toiled without getting to the big show. Considered one of the best at his position, White wanted a Super Bowl ring to top off a great career. Brett hoped to help take him there.

The team came out of the gate fast, winning at

Tampa Bay, 34–3, and at home against Philadelphia, 39–13. Next the Pack dismantled a good San Diego Chargers outfit, 42–10, and suddenly they were the talk of the league. The Packers had outscored their first three opponents by an outlandish margin of 115–26. They had turned the ball over just 5 times in 3 contests, compared to 13 takeaways of their opponents' turnovers. The ball club was rolling like a juggernaut.

Lambeau Field was quickly becoming the site of a full-time love-in. The loyal Packer fans had suffered for so many years after the Lombardi era that they embraced each and every member of the 1996 team. It became a Lambeau tradition that whenever a Packer scored a touchdown he would run through the end zone and leap into the stands to be pummeled with congratulatory claps on the back by the adoring fans.

Wideout Don Beebe, who had played on three Buffalo Bills Super Bowl teams, was amazed by what the Packers were doing. "It's scary," Beebe said. "This team is better than any Bills team I played on."

It was Brett who sounded a cautionary note—he knew there was still a long way to go. "We've only played three games," he said. "And the rest of our schedule is brutal."

Brett was right. A week later the team lost at Minnesota, 30–21. But maybe that was good, a wake-up call. No matter how good a team is, or thinks it is, it cannot afford to let down against any opponent.

Two more big wins followed, however: 31–10 at

Seattle, and 37–6 at Chicago. The Pack was even dominant on the road. And when they beat an elite opponent the next week, topping the 49ers, 23–20, in overtime, more and more observers were calling the Packers the team to beat in the NFL.

The victory over the Niners was not without a high price. Robert Brooks, the team's top receiver, suffered a severe knee injury and would be lost for the season. Great teams, however, must find ways to compensate for a loss. Soon afterward the team signed Andre Rison, a receiver with superstar talent, but a player who sometimes marched to his own beat. Rison, though, would make a major contribution once he learned the passing scheme.

The club won its next two, but in a 28–18 victory over Detroit, wide receiver Antonio Freeman, who had taken over from Brooks as Brett's primary deep threat, broke a bone in his forearm and would be lost for at least a month. Despite a league-best 8–1 record and a five-game winning streak, the team suddenly dropped two in a row and looked very ordinary.

Kansas City topped the Pack, 27–20. Then came the low point of the season, yet another loss to the Dallas Cowboys, 21–6. It seemed that no matter how good the Packers had become, they still couldn't put a dent in the Dallas armor. In addition, everyone who had touted the Pack as the league's powerhouse now took a second look.

"Green Bay, without a big-time threat at wide receiver and with no running attack to speak of, looked flawed, fragile, and frazzled" was the way one writer put it.

Injuries were part of the problem, and most teams, even the good ones, have a letdown at some point in the season. Brett was in the midst of another outstanding year. His numbers were close to those of his MVP season of 1995, and there was talk of a possible repeat performance. None of that really mattered, however; it was the team that was important.

Even so, there were those who felt that Brett was reverting to some of his old ways—not staying in the pocket long enough, trying to make his own plays, and using his strong arm to force the ball into coverage. Although the team won its next two games, beating mediocre St. Louis and Chicago teams, the Pack didn't look as dominating and impressive as it had earlier. So the game against the Denver Broncos suddenly loomed large.

The Packers were 10–3 and leading the NFC Central. But the Broncos now had the best record in the league. Led by quarterback John Elway, Denver was coming to Lambeau with a 12–1 mark, putting them atop the AFC West. Many observers had already tagged the game a Super Bowl preview—that's how big it was.

There was some good news on the Green Bay side of the ledger. Antonio Freeman was returning after missing four games because of his broken arm. With Andre Rison beginning to learn the system and with Freeman back, the Packers would once again have a deep passing game. Hopefully. And there was one other piece of encouraging news. The game was being played on the coldest football day in three years, with the wind chill bottoming out at 5 degrees below zero. Brett still had not lost a game with the temperature below 35 degrees.

Denver was resting its quarterback, John Elway, who had a sore hamstring. So the game might not have been as competitive as it could have. But for the Packers, there were other elements at work. In the first quarter Brett was hit hard by defensive end Alfred Williams and knocked dizzy. He would later say he was like a zombie in the first quarter, throwing a pair of interceptions.

So the game was close in the first half. In fact, the Packers had only a 6–3 lead with time running down in the second period. The ball was at the Denver 14 with just 17 seconds left. Brett dropped back to throw. The Broncos' 285-pound tackle, Michael Dean Perry, burst through looking for a sack. Brett sidestepped and stiff-armed the bigger Perry. Then he took a step back and, off-balance, rifled a pass to Freeman in the back of the end zone for a touchdown. The kick made it 13–3 at the half.

For Brett, that wasn't nearly a big enough lead. Early in the third period he got his offense together and urged them to continue playing as hard as they could.

"I told them to pour it on all through the second half," he said afterward, "because I wanted to make a statement. It wasn't so much directed at Denver, because I really don't think they cared about winning this game. But I wanted other teams to see what we can do when we have our house in order."

In that third quarter, Brett hooked up with Freeman on a brilliant 51-yard pass play for another score. After that, the Pack continued to roll and made it look easy. When it ended, Green Bay had a 41–6 victory that clinched their second straight NFC Central title. Brett completed 20 of 38 passes for 280 yards and 4 touchdowns. That gave him 35 TD passes for the year, the most in the league.

Other Packers were outstanding as well. Freeman returned from his injury to catch 9 passes for 175 big yards and 3 of the scores. Tight end Mark Chmura, who had missed three games with a sprained arch, caught 4 passes for 70 yards, while Keith Jackson also grabbed a touchdown toss. And the emerging Dorsey Levens gained 86 yards on 14 carries. In addition, the Green Bay defense recovered 3 fumbles. The defense had already produced 36 turnovers, compared with 16 the entire previous season. Once again it all seemed to be coming together.

"Early on in the season we were a confident, humbly arrogant team," Antonio Freeman said. "Then we came crashing back to earth. Now we're getting healthy, and if we can get our swagger back, we like our chances."

Brett was continuing to play in pain. He had torn two ankle ligaments in the Dallas game and said his left knee would need a "scoping" after the season. He also said he was bothered by injuries to "both hips, my back, a shoulder—you name it. This is as bad as it's ever been."

But he wasn't taking Vicodin. He was working

through it mostly on the strength of his strong will and a drive to reach the Super Bowl.

"He's playing angry," Coach Holmgren confirmed again. "He's had a chip on his shoulder all season."

From there the Packers closed out the regular season in fine style, winning their remaining two games against Detroit and Minnesota, 31–3 and 38–10. So they finished up resembling the same powerhouse team they had been at the beginning of the season. Their 13–3 record put them in a tie with Denver for best in league. The Pack was also the highest-scoring team in the NFL, with 456 points, while their defense gave up the fewest, 210. They averaged 28.5 points a game while holding their opponents to a 13.1 average.

A number of the Packers had great individual seasons. Defensive players Reggie White, Gilbert Brown, Leroy Butler, and Eugene Robinson were all standouts. On offense, Edgar Bennett ran for 899 yards, while Dorsey Levens gained 566. Despite missing four games, Antonio Freeman caught 56 passes for 933 yards and 9 touchdowns. Keith Jackson had 40 catches for 10 scores. All the other wide receivers, as well as the backs, contributed to a great passing attack.

Once again, though, the best individual season belonged to Brett Favre, who completed 325 of 543 passes for 3,899 yards and a league-leading 39 touchdown passes, breaking his NFC record of a year earlier. His completion percentage was 59.9, and he had just 13 passes picked off. His 95.8

quarterback efficiency rating was second in the league to Steve Young's 97.2. But Young had missed a number of games because of an injury and had just 14 TD tosses all year.

In addition, Brett's third straight great season elevated him to third place on the all-time quarterback list. His career 88.6 quarterback rating was topped only by Young and the great Joe Montana. Brett was now ahead of future Hall of Famers Dan Marino of Miami and Jim Kelly of Buffalo. He was beginning to carve out a niche for himself.

Then, during the first round of the playoffs (the Packers had a bye as divisional champs), Brett was named the league's Most Valuable Player for the second straight season, receiving 52 votes. John Elway was runner-up with 33½ votes. Brett was also the first-team All-Pro quarterback, again beating out Elway. But it was the MVP title that really excited him. He became just the second player in NFL history to win the prize two years in a row. The other was Joe Montana. The only other two-time winners (not in succession) were Steve Young and a couple of Hall of Fame legends, quarterback John Unitas and running back Jim Brown.

"It was more of a surprise this year than it was last year," Brett said. "And believe it or not, it felt much better this year than last year. I was really honored last year, but this year it was like a big weight was lifted off my shoulders. It was like, 'Whew, man, this is great.' This is another huge award [despite] a lot of bad things that have happened."

Brett admitted he had been under a great deal of pressure, what with the stigma of his Vicodin rehab, his brother's auto accident that cost the life of a longtime friend, and the pressure of trying to win a Super Bowl.

"I've heard it all this year, questions about me living up to what I've done in the past and putting up numbers similar to last year's. I thought it was going to be tough. To throw 33, 38, and 39 touchdowns back-to-back-to-back, I mean, that's hard. If [John Elway had] won it, I wouldn't have been disappointed. It's like a couple of years ago, I went to the Pro Bowl after throwing 24 interceptions, and the following year I threw 33 touchdowns, had a great year, and didn't go. That's the way I would have felt this year."

But as had been the case the year before, the MVP would mean next to nothing if the team didn't get through the playoffs and into the Super Bowl. That had been Brett's goal from the moment the team was defeated by Dallas in the NFC title game the year before.

Teammate Reggie White remembered the moment well. "Going home on the airplane, Brett shed a tear and made me a promise he would lead the team to the Super Bowl this year," White said.

Step one was the divisional game against the San Francisco 49ers. The Niners were 12–4 on the regular season, but were a wild-card entry when the 12–4 Carolina Panthers won the NFC West via a tiebreaker. The Niners then won their wild-card game and became the Packers' opponents. Green

Bay wanted a scenario where they would defeat the Niners, then face the Cowboys for the NFC title. Dallas had to play Carolina to get there.

They played the game at Lambeau in 34-degree temperatures, with a steady rain falling, a muddy field, and winds blowing at 20 miles per hour. It was Packer weather. The game was just over two minutes old when the Niners punted. The Pack's Desmond Howard fielded the ball at his own 29 and started upfield. He got two good blocks, broke a tackle, then cut to the outside and raced 71 yards for the game's first score. Chris Jacke's kick made it a 7–0 game.

Meanwhile the Niners had their own problems. Steve Young tried to go with a couple of broken ribs from the Eagles game the week before. He played two series, but the pain was so bad that he had to come out. Backup Elvis Grbac now had the game in his hands. Later in the first period the Pack struck again, and once more the action was started by Desmond Howard. His 46-yard punt return brought the ball to the San Francisco seven. Two plays later Brett rolled out and hit Andre Rison from 4 yards out for a score. The kick made it a 14–0 game, and that's the way it was after one.

Late in the second session, another Niner turnover gave Green Bay the ball at the SF 15. This time it took just three plays before Brett passed to Edgar Bennett from 10 yards out for still another score. That made it 21–0, the Packers firmly in control. Then San Francisco caught a break just before halftime when a punt glanced off a Packer and was recovered by the Niners at the Green Bay 26.

From there Grbac took six plays to get his team into the end zone. The kick made it 21–7. San Francisco kicked off to start the second half. Howard wasn't on the field; he was still in the locker room changing his wet pants. The kick squibbed under the reach of Don Beebe, and the Niners recovered the live ball at the 4-yard line. On the next play, Grbac ran it into the end zone. San Francisco had scored twice within 40 seconds and was suddenly back in the game at 21–14.

But on the sloppy field, the Packers responded. They started driving from their own 28 and moved the ball upfield with Edgar Bennett and Dorsey Levens doing the heavy-duty running in the mud. Some eleven plays later, the ball was at the three. Brett handed it off to Bennett again, and the running back leaped in the air. He was met head-on by safety Merton Hanks at the goal line and fumbled. When the bodies were unstacked, Antonio Freeman had recovered the ball in the end zone for a touchdown. The kick made it 28–14.

Meanwhile the Packers' defense was beginning to shut down the 49er attack. Then in the final session another recovered 49er fumble led to the final Packers score, Bennett running it in from the 11. Green Bay won the game convincingly, 35–14.

Brett had played a conservative game in the inclement weather, completing just 11 of 15 passes for 79 yards and one touchdown. Bennett gained 80 yards and Levens 46 to key the running game. Despite not putting up big numbers, Brett was only too happy to take the win.

"It was awful," Brett said of the weather. "The

more we played, the worse it got. But the bottom line is for us to go to New Orleans and win there. I could care less about throwing another touchdown pass. Stats are over for this year."

During the latter stages of the game the fans at Lambeau were chanting, "Dallas! Dallas! Dallas!" And safety Leroy Butler said what many of the Packers were thinking: "Until this organization beats Dallas, people aren't going to respect us. A lot of teams have a lot of respect for San Francisco, and to beat them the way we did, we'll gain respect. But maybe if Carolina beats Dallas, people will turn their set off. The thing they want to see is Dallas and Green Bay."

To the surprise of many, Carolina did pull off the upset. An expansion team in just its second season, the surprising Panthers upset the Cowboys, 26–17. So the Packers wouldn't get its chance to redeem themselves against the Cowboys. But they had better not get complacent. Carolina was a solid team, and if the Packers let down in the NFC title game, they wouldn't get their chance in New Orleans. So everyone pulled together and got ready to host the title game at Lambeau Field on January 12.

Once again it was Packer weather, icy cold with single-digit temperatures and a wind chill that reached 25 below, the kind of weather in which Brett Favre had never lost. The game was so important to Brett that he admitted he had trouble sleeping all week long. He was nervous, but he was also eager.

Coach Holmgren again admitted that Brett

sometimes was too pumped at the outset of a game. "Brett doesn't get tight," the coach said, "but he does get too excited sometimes."

That can result in early errors, and the game against Carolina was no exception. Six of Brett's first seven passes were off the mark, and he looked shaky. With 5:37 left in the first quarter and the Packers stuck at their own six, Brett dropped back to pass. He tried to throw a short slant to wideout Don Beebe. But veteran linebacker Sam Mills stepped in front of Beebe and picked the ball off, returning it to the two.

On the second play from scrimmage, Carolina quarterback Kerry Collins flipped a 3-yard TD toss to fullback Howard Griffith, and the Panthers were on the board. The extra point made it a 7–0 game. Then late in the period, the Packers began driving from their own 27. Sparked by a 35-yard run by Dorsey Levens, the Packers had the ball at the Panthers' 29 when the quarter ended.

Brett stood over center to start the second period. He called signals, dropped back, and lofted a perfect 29-yard scoring pass to Levens in the end zone. The kick tied the game at 7–7. But on Green Bay's next drive, Brett fumbled and the Panthers recovered. Seven plays later John Kasay kicked a 22-yard field goal and Carolina had regained the lead, 10–7.

Now was the time for the Packers to make a statement. They didn't want Carolina to get too confident. Led by Brett, the offense began a nearly 8-minute drive that covered 71 yards in 15 plays. Brett hit on several key passes on the drive, finally connecting with Freeman from the 6 for the score. The kick gave Green Bay the lead at 14–10. When Carolina tried to come back following the kickoff, the Packers quickly intercepted a pass at the Green Bay 38.

With time running down, Brett flashed brilliance. He connected on a 23-yard pass to Rison, then followed it quickly with a 25-yard strike to Freeman. That allowed Chris Jacke to come on and boot a 31-yard field goal with just 10 seconds left. The Packers had scored 10 points in 38 seconds and left the field with a 17–10 halftime lead.

The second half was all Packers. Green Bay moved the ball through the air and on the ground, coming away with a 30–13 victory. They had made it back to the Super Bowl after 29 years. Brett was 19 of 29 for 292 yards and a touchdown. He had plenty of help. Bennett ran for 99 yards, Levens for 88. In addition, Levens caught 5 passes for 117 yards to complete his best day as a Packer.

"[Reaching the Super Bowl] is the biggest story in a long time," Brett said an hour after the game. "We've had to overcome so many obstacles, and I think people were moved by our quest. This team has been kind of like potluck, a mixture of the good, the bad, and the ugly. I've done a lot of thinking, crying, cheering, and hugging over the past year, and it all began that day in Dallas."

That was the day the Pack lost to the Cowboys in the NFC title game the previous year. Now the yearlong quest was one game away from being completed. It had surely been a team effort, but many singled out Brett Favre as the key.

"I think [the Packers] are a better football team," said Carolina quarterback Kerry Collins. "They won the fundamental part of the game. They ran the ball on us, and they stopped the run. And Brett Favre is as good a quarterback as has been around in a long time. He's a very heady quarterback, and he makes the big plays. Their defense is similar to [that of] the 49ers, but Brett just takes them to another level."

More praise came from another Green Bay legend. Bart Starr was the quarterback of Vince Lombardi's championship teams in the 1960s. After the game he was asked what he thought about Brett.

The Hall of Famer didn't hesitate to answer. "He's just a sensational young quarterback," Starr said. "I love watching him play. He has grown to execute a system expertly. He is extremely talented. I love his courage, but his mobility combined with everything else I think is what sets him apart. His ability to move and throw on the run, his arm strength enables him to eat teams alive. I have never seen a quarterback at his young age as good as he is."

So the stage was set. In the Super Bowl the Packers would be meeting the AFC champion New England Patriots. The Pats, under Coach Bill Parcells, defeated the upstart Jacksonville Jaguars, 20–6, in the AFC title game. A week earlier the Jags had upset the AFC favorite Denver Broncos, opening the door for the Patriots.

New England was 11–5 during the regular season and the second-highest scoring team in the league behind the Packers. The Pats' offense was led by the strong-armed Drew Bledsoe, who had thrown for more than 4,000 yards with 27 touchdowns. He had a pair of outstanding receivers in wideout Terry Glenn, who had 90 catches for 1,132 yards and 6 touchdowns; and tight end Ben Coates, who had 62 passes and 9 TDs. Running back Curtis Martin had gained 1,152 yards and scored 14 times during the regular season. So the Patriots could put points on the board, though their defense wasn't considered on a par with that of Green Bay.

Coming into Super Bowl XXXI, the Packers were 13½-point favorites. The NFC had won 12 straight titles, and the Pack didn't want to break the string. In the two weeks between the conference championship games and the Super Bowl, there was plenty of hype. Much of it centered around Brett.

One writer put it this way: "When the Superdome lights go on Sunday for Super Bowl XXXI, the glare will be . . . shining the brightest on Favre . . . who has ascended to such prominence that it is no longer enough to define him as the best player in the game. He is also the most compelling, a riveting mixture of vulnerability and stardom."

Patriots linebacker Chris Slade showed the kind of respect the other players had for Brett's toughness when he said, "He's like a linebacker playing quarterback. The more you hit him, the better he seems to play. The guy is dangerous."

Brett, of course, was bombarded with questions

from the hordes of media who descended on New Orleans. He tried to answer all of them patiently and accurately. He finally summed up his feelings about how he appreciated being in New Orleans for the biggest game of his life.

"In order to experience the highs and to be in the position I'm in today, I had to go through a lot of lows," he explained. "I think a lot of people can say that. It's not rosy for everybody. As you go through the tough times, you're mad, you're sad, you're angry, all of that. But then you're in a position like this and you're in the Super Bowl, you appreciate it. You really wouldn't if you didn't go through the hard times."

Brett had certainly traveled a sometimes rocky road, but he triumphed. One interesting statistic was offered among the many. Over a three-year span, Brett Favre had the best touchdown-to-interception ratio of any NFL quarterback who had ever played the game. From 1994 to 1996 he had thrown for 110 touchdowns and been intercepted just 40 times. That meant he had thrown 70 more touchdown passes than interceptions. Dan Marino was next with 122 and 61, for a plus-61, followed by Steve Young with 89 and 53, a plus-56. That was just another example of how good Brett Favre had become.

But numbers don't mean anything once the game begins. Some 72,301 fans jammed the Louisiana SuperDome in New Orleans while millions more watched on television. New England got the ball first and went nowhere. The Pats punted to the Packers. Desmond Howard returned it 33 yards, almost to midfield. Green Bay had the ball at their own 46 on just their second play from scrimmage when Brett dropped back to pass. This time he wasn't too excited to throw well. He unleashed a long pass downfield. Andre Rison was behind the defense in full stride. When he reached up, the ball was right there, and he caught it as he streaked into the end zone, completing a 54-yard touchdown play. The extra point gave the Packers a quick 7–0, lead. It looked as if the rout was on.

Two plays after the Pats' kickoff return, Drew Bledsoe threw the ball in the direction of Terry Glenn. Cornerback Doug Evans intercepted the pass, and four plays later Chris Jacke booted a 37-yard field goal to up the Packer lead to 10–0.

But the Patriots wouldn't quit. On the next series, Bledsoe drove his team downfield, tossing a short TD pass to Keith Byars. The kick cut the lead to 10–7. Maybe it would be a ball game after all. When the Packers couldn't move the ball, the Patriots got it back again. Once again they began attacking the Green Bay defense with play-action passes and screens. Bledsoe hit Terry Glenn with a 44-yard bomb to key another TD drive. The score came on a 4-yarder to tight end Coates. Green Bay fans were in shock. The first quarter wasn't yet over, and the Patriots had a 14–10 lead.

"We were completely baffled," said safety Leroy Butler. "We were missing tackles, they were flying right past us, and they were pushing us around. No one had pushed us around all year, and they were killing us, doing stuff we hadn't seen before. It was a great game plan."

If the Packers were to prove they were a great team, they would have to step up. They decided to change the defense and go after Bledsoe. And it would be up to Brett Favre to get the Packer offense in gear once again. Since taking a 10–0 lead, Green Bay's offense had gained just 2 yards in three series. But at the outset of the second quarter, Brett and the Pack made a statement.

The ball was at their own 19. Brett dropped back and looked down the right side. He saw the fleet Antonio Freeman working one-on-one with strong safety Lawyer Milloy and fired another long bomb. It was right on the mark. Freeman grabbed it on the run and streaked all the way to the end zone. The 81-yard touchdown was the longest from scrimmage in Super Bowl history, and it gave the Packers the lead at 17–14. It also seemed to take some of the heart out of the Patriots.

Before the period ended, Howard returned a punt 34 yards, helping to set up a 31-yard Jacke field goal for a 20–14 lead. Then, just two plays later, Pack safety Mike Prior picked off another Bledsoe pass, leading to a Green Bay drive that ended with Brett taking it over himself from 2 yards out. The kick made it a 27–14 game at the half, and that just about did it.

The Patriots tried to rally in the third quarter. With 3:27 left in the period, they culminated a drive with Curtis Martin running it over from 18 yards out. The kick made it 27–21, with everyone wondering if the momentum would change again.

Desmond Howard made sure it wouldn't. The speedy 180-pounder took the ensuing kickoff at his own 10-yard line. He burst right up the middle and was past the first line of Patriot defenders in a breath. He then made one move and was in the clear, sprinting untouched to the end zone for a backbreaking 90-yard kickoff return. The Packers decided to go for a 2-point conversion, and Brett flipped a short pass to Mark Chmura, giving them a 35–21 lead.

In the fourth period the Green Bay defense took over. Led by Reggie White, who had three sacks in the final 18 minutes, the Packer defenders refused to let Bledsoe and the Pats get anything started. Neither team scored in the final session. The 35–21 score turned out to be the final.

Brett had played an outstanding game, hitting 14 of 27 passes for 246 yards and 2 scores. Levens ran for 61 yards, Bennett for 40. But it was little Desmond Howard who set up 2 scores with punt returns and had a 90-yard kickoff return for another score. He later won the Most Valuable Player award. No one argued with the choice.

The Packers had done it. They were champions of the world. Brett hugged Reggie White, who had waited so long for this moment. Brett and Coach Holmgren embraced as well. They had been through so much together.

"It's great to win this anywhere," Brett said, "but so close to home makes it special. I don't know what else I've got to do. I've won everything I possibly can. Winning the Super Bowl feels better than the MVP."

Later, as the celebration continued in the Superdome, Brett talked about the ups and downs of the past year, knowing how uncertain the future might be.

"Through everything," he said, "I really believed I'd be here today. Right here . . . talking about being world champions. My best friend is gone forever [in the car accident with Brett's brother]. Trouble never seems to be far away, and the future won't be all rosy. But they can't take this away from me. Years from now, hopefully, people will remember how Brett Favre fought through such adversity. There will be other players and coaches then. But I know this: we etched our place in history today."

Chapter 11

The March to Greatness

The Pack was all the way back. Green Bay's Super Bowl triumph was like a breath of fresh air. The Cowboys and 49ers had dominated for so long—they had won the last four—that everyone was ready for someone new. Not only did the Packers evoke memories of Vince Lombardi's time, but the personal stories of Brett Favre and Reggie White—the club's two leaders—caught the fancy of the public.

By now, of course, many were beginning to call Brett the number one quarterback in the game. Veterans such as Steve Young, Dan Marino, and John Elway were in the twilight of their careers. Now Brett's numbers and style were being favorably compared to the likes of Troy Aikman, Drew Bledsoe, and Jim Harbaugh, the best of the young veterans. There were also some promising youngsters, such as Mark Brunell, Jeff Blake, Brad Johnson, and Trent Dilfer. But as of 1996, Brett was being looked upon as the top guy.

Even the advertising world had discovered him. Up to this point, Brett had only a handful of off-field endorsements, but that was about to change. Mike Levine of the New York–based Athletes & Artists talent agency felt that Brett was about to make a big splash. "His value has jumped tremendously," Levine said. "I think he has to be one of the most valuable marketing properties around right now. With back-to-back MVPs and a Super Bowl title, the world's at his feet."

Brett began appearing with a number of other celebrity athletes in a "Got milk?" ad that shows various athletes with milk mustaches. It wouldn't be long before Brett began endorsing even more products.

Then in July of 1997 Brett's star status was further enhanced when the Packers rewrote his contract. Back in 1994 he had signed a five-year, $19 million pact that still had two years to go. The new deal was a seven-year extension reportedly worth between $42 and $48 million, which included a $12 million signing bonus. Packers general manager Ron Wolf said the new pact made Brett, at age twenty-seven, "the highest-paid player in the history of professional football."

As for Brett, his self-confidence was at an all-time high. "I've proven over the last couple of years that I have been the best player in the league," he said, stating a fact rather than making a cocky boast. "This just shows me that the Packers and Ron felt the same way."

There were a few changes in the team as the preseason got under way. The Packers were chosen early to repeat, and the big-name players were confident.

"I like our chances," Brett said. "They'll all be shootin' for us, but you should hear the guys talking at camp. There's so much confidence, so much belief."

Defensive end Reggie White, the team's co-leader with Brett, echoed similar thoughts. "I have a feeling," he said. "Of course, you never like to talk about this kind of thing before the season starts. But there's just something about this team and this franchise. It's like we're meant to win."

Some key players were gone. Tight end Keith Jackson, backup quarterback Jim McMahon, and defensive end Sean Jones had all retired. Andre Rison and Desmond Howard, the Super Bowl MVP, left via free agency. But the team signed the solid Steve Bono as a backup for Brett, as well as former All-Pro linebacker Seth Joyner. They also had a new place kicker in Ryan Longwell.

The team's first preseason game, a 20–0 victory over Miami, proved a costly one. Running back Edgar Bennett suffered a torn Achilles tendon and would be lost for the season. That meant Dorsey Levens, who'd had a fine 1996 season alternating with Bennett, would now become the featured back. There was some question whether Levens could handle the increased workload. But overcoming injuries is something all great teams must do. The one player the team could least afford to lose, obviously, was Brett Favre. He was already looking like his old self and playing extremely well.

There was more good news as the team prepared to open the 1997 season and the defense of its championship. Wide receiver Robert Brooks, lost to a serious knee injury the previous October, had made a wondrous recovery and was again ready to go full speed. When healthy, Brooks and Antonio Freeman gave the Pack and Brett one of the best pass-catching tandems in the league.

Green Bay opened its season by hosting the Chicago Bears at Lambeau Field. The Packers rolled to a 38–24 victory with Brett hitting on 15 of 22 passes for 226 yards and 2 scores. One of them was an 18-yarder to Robert Brooks, who showed little rust from his inactivity. Ryan Longwell kicked three field goals in his first game as a Packer, and Levens played very well as the featured running back. Business as usual for the defending champs.

In fact, some experts thought the Packers were so good they might go through the season undefeated. A week later in Philadelphia, however, that talk stopped abruptly. The Eagles walked away with an almost shocking 10–9 victory. The Packers were sloppy. Dropped passes, penalties, and sloppy execution added to their not getting it going. Brett was blitzed and harassed all afternoon. He tried to drive the team at the end, but Longwell, who had kicked three more field goals, missed a 28-yarder that could have won it.

The next week the Packers went up against the

Miami Dolphins and came away with a hard-fought 23–18 victory. Levens ran for a career high 121 yards and was looking more and more like a coming star. But for the second week in a row, Brett was a marked man and took a fearful beating from the hard-charging Dolphin defenders. He winced in pain when he sat down for the postgame press conference.

"This is the most sore I've been all year" was the first thing he said. He knew teams were coming after him and would continue to do so.

"I was saying toward the end of the game that it's going to be this way every week," he told reporters. "People are asking why we're not blowing teams out like we did early last year, but that stuff is over with. Beating the Packers gives you a chance to boast, to stick out your chest. We're not going to sneak up on anybody."

A week later Brett caught fire against the Vikings. He tied a career best by throwing 5 touchdown passes as the Pack won, 38–32. The troubling part was that Green Bay had a 31–7 halftime lead and then had to scramble for the victory.

"I'd be lying to you if I said I wasn't worried," Brett said. "When we were up 31–7, everyone was kind of coasting. We were talking about what we were going to do this week, where we're playing golf."

The Minnesota game was a personal milestone for Brett. Among his 5 TD tosses was the 153rd of his career, breaking Bart Starr's all-time Packers record. But at this point individual achievement didn't matter. The Packers as a team were struggling, and it showed again the following week against division rival Detroit. Led by the great running back, Barry Sanders, the Lions upset the Pack, 26–15, dropping Green Bay's record to a mediocre 3–2.

Brett was again under heavy pressure. He was 22 of 43 for 295 yards. But he had just a single TD toss and was intercepted three times. Sanders ran for 139 yards, and Green Bay just couldn't seem to get it in high gear. The Pack trailed 17–9 at the half, then cut the lead to 17–15, and didn't score again. The Lions prevailed in the final session.

Brett was so upset that he declined to talk to reporters after the game. But the following Wednesday he finally explained why. He said that he was upset by the tactics that the defenses seemed to be using; he claimed that a number of defensive players had been going after his knees.

"I understand this is a tough game, but there are times guys go after your legs and you watch it on film and you know it's totally uncalled for," he said. "I respect this game the way people play it, but when you kind of go out of the lines of the rules, it's not right. You can end a guy's career."

These were not the complaints of a whiner. Brett Favre was known as one of the toughest guys in the league, a gamer, a guy known for playing through pain. Hit him legally, no matter how hard, and he would get up and congratulate you. It was the borderline-illegal hits, the ones designed to put a guy out of action, that bothered him. And rightly so. The overriding concern, however, was getting the team back on track. Coming into Lambeau the following week were the Tampa Bay Buccaneers. The Bucs were off to a 5–0 start and had a two-game lead over the Pack in the NFC Central.

Somehow the Pack survived, but still didn't look like last year's juggernaut. Tampa Bay took a 3–0 lead in the first quarter. Then Green Bay erupted for 21 second-quarter points. Brett started it with a 31-yard touchdown pass to Antonio Freeman. The next TD came when defensive end Gabe Wilkins picked off a Trent Dilfer screen pass and rambled 77 yards for the score. Then late in the session Brett hit Freeman again, this time from 6 yards out. The halftime lead was 21–3.

In the second half the Packers had to hang on again. Tampa Bay scored twice while Brett and his offense were shut down. The final was 21–16, not pretty, but a victory. Brett was 21 of 31 for 191 yards. Not one of his best games, either. The questions about the team remained. They remained a week later when the Pack could beat the winless Bears by only a single point, 24–23.

Then came a solid win, a repeat of last year's Super Bowl. The Packers beat New England, 28–10, with Brett throwing for three scores and leading the team on three long scoring drives. Wins over Detroit (20–10) and St. Louis (17–7) followed, but neither was close to a blowout. And the Rams had an abysmal 2–8 record. By contrast, Green Bay was 8–2, but the Pack just wasn't dominating, even the weaker teams. For that reason, the next game, with the Indianapolis Colts, was a turning point. The Colts hadn't won a single game all year. The fear was that the Packers might look past them. Waiting in the wings the following week would be the Dallas Cowboys.

The Indianapolis game was a shoot-out, and turned out to be an embarrassment for the proud champions. Brett was considered the best quarterback in the game, yet his performance was being matched by a little-known backup, Paul Justin. Both clubs were eating up the yards in big chunks. At the half, Green Bay had a 28–27 lead, with Brett having thrown a pair of TD passes. The scoring slowed in the second half, but the game remained close.

The Colts had a 38–31 lead in the fourth quarter when Brett drove the Pack downfield. He then threw his third TD pass, hitting Freeman from 26 yards out with 5:19 remaining. Longwell's kick tied the game at 38–38. If the Packer defense could stop the Colts, Brett would have a chance to win it.

But instead, it was the Colts who played like champions. Justin drove his team 72 yards in the final 5:19, allowing Cary Blanchard to kick the game-winning 20-yard field goal as time ran out. Indianapolis had won it, 41–38. Brett completed 18 of 25 passes for 363 yards and three scores. But he also committed three turnovers (two on intercepts) that led to 17 points for the Colts. It was a devastating defeat.

"It's tough to lose any game," Brett said. "I tip my hat to the Colts. I knew there was no team in this league that could go without a win. Unfortunately, it was against us. There's no excuse for losing. We felt we should have won. We put up a lot of points . . . we just didn't get the job done."

So while the Packers were at 8–3 on the year, there were questions. The team didn't look as dominant as it had in 1996. Now they had to prepare for the Cowboys, the team they had hoped to meet in the playoffs the previous season. They didn't, so this game loomed very large. Dallas was struggling somewhat, coming in with a 6–5 record and a playoff spot in doubt. So the game was big for them as well.

Despite the close games and a couple of unexpected losses, Brett was beginning to put together another big year. He already had 23 touchdown passes, tied for the league lead, and his 2,776 passing yards were second in the NFL. In addition, Antonio Freeman and Robert Brooks were the top pass-catching tandem in the NFC, having combined for 99 catches, 1,534 yards, and 12 scores.

The game against Dallas turned out to be a turning point in the season for the Packers. The first half was close. Despite 60,111 cheering fans at Lambeau Field, Green Bay could manage only a 10–10 tie at the half. But after intermission, the Packers suddenly returned to their championship form. They scored every time they touched the football. With Dorsey Levens running through and around the Dallas defense, and Brett throwing for 3 second-half touchdowns, the Packers romped to a 45–17 victory. They had finally ended the Cowboys hex.

Levens set a new Green Bay single-game rushing

record by gaining 190 yards on 33 carries. Brett completed 22 of 35 passes for 203 yards and 4 touchdown passes. His old college rival, Deion Sanders, picked one off in the first half and ran it back for a touchdown. But after the game, the man called Prime Time was quick to praise the Green Bay quarterback. "He's a great player," Deion said. "When you have a Brett Favre, you can do things. The way he runs around back there, making plays, you don't teach that."

Packers tackle Ross Verba said that Brett was the driving force behind the victory. "Brett just wouldn't settle for less today," Verba said. "Each time he came into the huddle he said, 'C'mon, keep pounding them.' He's the leader of the boat, and that's what I love about him. He gets you excited, and I play better when someone's on my case. Can you imagine a quarterback telling his offensive linemen to pound people? It's what we dream of."

Brett, too, was happy to beat Dallas. "It feels about like I thought it would," Brett said. "It's great to finally beat these guys. It's a shame it took so long."

In the second half the Packers had converted 9 of 9 third-down plays, and 13 of 17 for the game. It was such an overwhelming victory that it seemed to set the tone for the remainder of the season. After the Dallas win, the Packers ran the table, winning their final four games in impressive fashion. They finished the year with a third straight NFC Central Division title and a record identical to that of the season before, 13–3.

Brett had put together another outstanding season. By the numbers, he completed 304 of 513 passes for 3,867 yards, most in the NFC. He also threw for an NFL best 35 touchdowns and had 16 passes picked off. Along the way he became the first quarterback in NFL history to have 30 or more TD passes in 4 consecutive seasons. And once again he started all 16 games.

Levens had proved to be an All-Pro-caliber runner in his first year as the featured back. He was second in the NFC behind the great Barry Sanders with 1,435 yards in 329 carries. It was a workhorse season for him. Antonio Freeman had his best year with 81 catches for 1,243 yards and 12 touchdowns. There was plenty of support as well, with the Packers the second-highest-scoring team in the league behind the AFC Denver Broncos.

With their strong finish, the Packers were made immediate favorites to defend their Super Bowl title. Then, as the playoffs got under way, it was time for the Most Valuable Player award. The announcement was somewhat of a surprise. For just the second time in NFL annals, there was a tie for the award. The co-winners were Detroit running back Barry Sanders . . . and Brett Favre!

That's right. Brett had won an unprecedented third MVP in a row. He was not only the first to win three in a row but also the first to win the honor three times. Sanders had also had a great season, becoming the third running back in history to gain more than 2,000 yards. Though the two tied with 18 votes each, sharing the award made it no less prestigious.

"I felt, up until about three weeks ago that, first of all, I wouldn't win it," Brett said. "I felt like Barry Sanders and [Denver running back] Terrell Davis had the upper hand. But Barry is an amazing player. I'm honored to be voted again and to be with him. To be up on a pedestal with him is amazing."

Sanders had similar sentiments and praise. "I guess it puts me in elite company," he explained. "I'm glad [Brett] let me share it with him this year, because the last couple of years he's taken it for himself.

"He reminds me a lot of Michael Jordan. No matter how successful he's been, he's still always the most competitive person on the field. Outside of his incredible talent and everything, he's always just really competitive."

Chapter 12

The Playoffs and Beyond

Brett was certainly compiling an amazing record. Now all that remained for him to do in the 1997 season was to help his team win a second successive Super Bowl. That would be the icing on the cake. Once again the Packers drew a first-round bye. In the divisional playoff, the Pack had to face the Tampa Bay Buccaneers. The Bucs had finished second in the NFC West with a 10–6 mark to earn a wild card. They won their wild-card game and would challenge the Pack once more.

The game was played in the cold at Lambeau Field on January 4, 1998. Brett's cold-weather record at Lambeau was now an incredible 22–0. He wasn't about to have that blemished, especially in the playoffs. The Bucs were a solid, competitive team, but the Packers methodically took them apart, both offensively and defensively.

When it ended, Green Bay had a solid 21–7 victory. Dorsey Levens set a Packers playoff record with 112 yards rushing, while Brett completed 15 of 28 passes for 190 yards and a score. He did have two picked off and was sacked four times, but he was throwing so hard that five of his passes were dropped. Several times during the game, Brett got into shoving and jawing matches with Bucs star defensive tackle Warren Sapp, who chased him all afternoon.

After the game, he laughed about the confrontation. "It's just part of the game," Brett said. "Warren kept telling me he was going to get me, and I told him he was welcome to try. I enjoy that kind of stuff."

Always the competitor, Brett welcomed any kind of challenge. The next challengers would be the San Francisco 49ers. The Niners would be the Pack's opponent in the NFC championship game. This year it would be played at Candlestick Park in San Francisco, however, so Brett wouldn't have the advantage of the frozen tundra at Lambeau. There was another element to the game. The 49ers had a rookie coach in Steve Mariucci—the same Steve Mariucci who had been the quarterback coach at Green Bay and had played a big role in Brett's development.

Although Brett acknowledged how grateful he was for the part Mariucci had played in his development, he knew the most important thing for both of them was winning the game.

"It makes for a great story," Brett said, "but the bottom line is we gotta go out there and kick their tail, and they gotta go out there and kick our tail. I love Steve [Mariucci] to death, and I'm sure Mike [Holmgren] loves Steve to death. But it's three hours of barroom brawl, and they know it and we know it."

Mariucci said knowing Brett so well didn't make it any easier to prepare to play against him. "[Knowing him] makes it even scarier" was the way Mariucci put it. "People keep asking me about his strengths and weaknesses. . . . I don't know many weaknesses."

Brett's teammates always felt confident when they saw number 4 trot onto the field. Tackle Santana Dotson spoke for all of them when he said, "I think [Brett's] the best quarterback, definitely the best player on the field, whenever he shows up. He's one of the most aggressive quarterbacks I've ever been around."

So Brett's teammates were always ready to go to war beside him. Those who knew him best said he valued his growing reputation as the best quarterback in the game. That was why he always enjoyed going up against the likes of Troy Aikman of the Cowboys and Steve Young of the 49ers. "I just want to be the quarterback everyone expects me to be," Brett said prior to the game.

The NFC title game was between two teams that had identical 13–3 records during the regular season. Both had outstanding quarterbacks, good supporting players, and a tough defense. The Niners didn't have a running back to match Dorsey Levens, though, and they were missing their all-time-great pass receiver, Jerry Rice, due to injury. But the game was still expected to be competitive.

It was—but only to a degree. The Packers didn't blow the Niners away, but they were better in enough areas to win slowly and convincingly.

In the first period the two teams slugged it out almost to a stalemate. The only score was Ryan Longwell's 19-yard field goal with 2:48 left in the period. Then, at the outset of the second period, the Packers made their first break. Eugene Robinson intercepted a Steve Young pass not only to stop a Niner drive but also to return it 58 yards to the San Francisco 28. Two plays later Brett hit Antonio Freeman on a crossing pattern at the 20, and the speedy wide receiver took it all the way to the end zone. Longwell's point after made it a 10–0 game. The two teams traded field goals before the half, and Green Bay went to intermission with a 13–3 lead.

The second half was more of the same. After a scoreless third period, the Packers went to work again. A 25-yard Longwell field goal made it 16–3 with 5:04 left. Minutes later a Niner gamble failed when Young was sacked on a fourth-down play deep in his own territory. Two plays later, Levens ran it in from the 5. The kick made it 23–3 with just 3:10 left. It was, in essence, over. Only a 95-yard kickoff return by Chuck Levy with 2:52 left prevented the Niners from being completely embarrassed.

Green Bay had won a second straight NFC championship, 23–10, and had totally dominated all areas of the game. Levens again went over 100 yards with 114 on 27 carries, while Brett hit on 16 of 27 passes for 222 yards and a touchdown. The Packer machine was now ready for a second assault on the Super Bowl.

It wasn't long before the story line for Super Bowl XXXII was set. In the AFC, the Denver Broncos had emerged as the champions with a 24–21 victory over the Pittsburgh Steelers in the title game. The Broncos had been 12–4 in the regular season and had made it to the playoffs as a wild card. But en route to the Super Bowl they defeated the Jacksonville Jaguars, 42–17; the Kansas City Chiefs, 14–10; and then the Steelers. The Chiefs had been 13–3 in the regular season and were the AFC West winners. Yet the Broncos topped them.

The Denver story revolved around 37-year-old quarterback John Elway. Elway had been a top quarterback since 1983 and was now considered an all-time great, a future Hall of Famer. Yet there was one thing missing from his résumé. Elway had never won the Super Bowl, despite taking the Broncos there on three previous occasions. That was the blot on his record. In each of his previous appearances in the super game his team had lost badly and he hadn't performed well. The game was being played up as his last chance at Super Bowl redemption.

In addition to Elway's strong throwing arm, the Broncos had one of the best running backs in the league. Terrell Davis was second only to Barry Sanders in rushing and had gained 184 yards in the AFC title tilt with Pittsburgh. He was definitely a big-time runner who could carry a team. So Denver had an explosive offense. Their defense wasn't considered as good as the Packers', but it wasn't bad, either. In addition, the AFC had now lost 13 straight Super Bowls to NFC teams. Denver wanted to break that hex, but Green Bay, of course, wanted to continue it.

There were two weeks between the conference championship and the Super Bowl, which was being held in San Diego. During that time, much of the focus was on the quarterbacks. Most experts, however, felt that even if Elway played an outstanding game, Brett would find a way to be better.

One writer described Brett as "Superman on Super Sunday." He went on, "No one knows how to stop him, because no one has seen a quarterback like this. He can kill you with his brain now as well as his brawn. . . . No one knows what Favre will do on any given play . . . because Favre often does not know himself."

Others said essentially the same thing. "You can't [stop him]," said Eagles coach Ray Rhodes. "That's the thing about Brett Favre; you can't plan for him. He can improvise at any time and make an ugly play pretty."

Bucs coach Tony Dungy echoed those thoughts. "You gotta hope he has an off day," Dungy said. "It seems like when he needs to make big plays, he makes them. We haven't figured out a way [to stop him] yet. We're still looking."

So while sentiment might have been with Elway and the Broncos, reason seemed to be on the side of the Packers. Even Brett's father marveled at how far he'd come. "It's amazing to me, all the things that have gone on, how he has been so successful, and how he can keep his mind on what he's doing," Irvin Favre said. "I think I've figured it out, though. Football is an escape for Brett.

"He always plays well in big games. He knows what's on the line. If you're any kind of leader, you know what you have to do to win. . . . If you're a leader, you don't mind putting yourself on the line and going out and doing it."

Brett was well aware that he was beginning to carve his own place in NFL history. He has already said he wanted to be the third quarterback to win four Super Bowls (Terry Bradshaw and Joe Montana were the others).

"I would like to do things that have never been done in the game," Brett said. "I've already done good and bad things that have never been done in this game. That's part of it. But I've had a lot of fun doing it. And I still have the desire to do everything I possibly can do. I want to win another MVP. I want to win another Super Bowl."

Then, however, Brett showed his other side, that he understood the frustration John Elway had lived with. "If we should lose the game," he said, "I will still be happy for John."

Many already seemed to consider Brett a seasoned veteran, on a par with the Marinos, Youngs, and Elways of the league. But as one writer pointed out, there was a fundamental difference: "The scariest part is that Brett has thrown for 112 touchdowns and more than 12,000 yards in just the past three years. And he's only twenty-eight years old."

Finally the hype was over and the game was at hand. It was a beautiful sunny day at San Diego as the Packers took the opening kickoff back to their own 24-yard line. Brett and the offense then came out on the field and made it look easy. They drove downfield in just eight plays, with all three offensive stars getting into the act.

Brett hit Antonio Freeman twice on slant-ins, threading the needle, each one good for 13 yards. Levens showed his power and skills in gaining 11 yards on one run and 13 on another. Finally the Pack had a first down on the Denver 22, and Brett dropped back to pass again. This time he lofted a perfect pass toward the rear of the end zone. It dropped into the arms of Antonio Freeman between two Bronco defenders for a touchdown. It was a perfectly thrown ball, and Longwell's kick made it a 7–0 game with 10:58 still remaining in the opening session. To many observers, it looked as if another NFC rout was on.

But the Broncos quickly showed that they weren't ready to lie down and let the Packers roll over them. Elway came out and drove his team 58 yards on 10 plays for the tying touchdown. Terrell Davis quickly established the Denver running game by scampering for 27 yards on one run, then scoring from the one.

Suddenly the Packers looked like mere mortals. On their next two possessions they gained just 17 yards and turned the ball over twice. Denver's blitzing defense forced Brett to hurry a pass that sailed over Robert Brooks's head into the arms of safety Tyrone Braxton, giving the Broncos the ball at the Green Bay 45. Elway then drove the Broncos 45 yards in eight plays. Davis's 16-yard run and 9-yard pass to tight end Shannon Sharpe highlighted the drive. Elway took it in himself from the one. The kick gave Denver a surprise 14–7 lead.

A short time later a blind-side blitz caused Brett to fumble the ball, with Denver recovering at the Packers' 33. The Broncos couldn't move the ball, but Jason Elam came on to boot a 51-yard field goal to increase the lead to 17–7. Now the pressure was on the Packers. With just 7:38 left before the half, a Denver punt rolled dead on the Green Bay 5-yard line. Brett then came out and began leading his club on a long 95-yard march.

It was a controlled drive, featuring Levens on the ground and Favre throwing to Freeman and tight end Mark Chmura. The drive took 17 plays and consumed nearly all the time remaining in the half. With just 12 seconds left, Brett hit Chmura in the right corner of the end zone, tossing the ball perfectly over the heads of two Denver defenders. Longwell's kick closed the gap to 17–14 at the half.

So it was a real game. Terrell Davis missed a good part of the second quarter after being hit in the head and developing a migraine headache. But he returned in the third quarter to become a major factor. Green Bay tied the game early in the period after recovering a Denver fumble. Longwell wound up kicking a 27-yard field goal. But before the period ended, Denver took the lead once again.

The Broncos drove 92 yards on 13 plays, with Davis eating up yardage on the ground and Elway hitting a pair of key passes to wideout Ed McCaffrey. It was also becoming apparent that Denver's offensive line was beginning to wear down the Packers' defensive front four. The 7-minute drive ended with Davis going over from the one. The kick made it a 24–17 game with just 34 seconds left in the third period.

When Antonio Freeman fumbled the ensuing kickoff, it looked as if Denver had caught a major break. But on the next play Green Bay's Eugene Robinson intercepted Elway's pass in the end zone and returned it to the 15-yard line. That opened the door for Brett to lead his team on an 85-yard clutch drive that took just four plays. It was helped by a 25-yard pass interference penalty against Denver's Darrien Gordon.

Finally Brett hit Antonio Freeman from the 13 for another score. Longwell's extra point tied the game once more at 24–24, with 13:32 still left in the game. The contest now became a battle for survival, one of the most competitive Super Bowl games of recent years.

Finally, with minutes left, Denver got the ball at the Packers' 49. Helped by a face mask penalty against the Packers, Elway and Davis led the Broncos downfield. With just 1:45 left, Davis ran the ball in from the one. The kick gave Denver the lead again, 31–24. Brett Favre would have just one chance to produce yet another miracle.

The kick was run back to the Green Bay 30. Brett now had 1:39 to take his team 70 yards. At first it looked as if he might do just that. He hit Levens with a quick shovel pass that the running back turned into a 22-yard gain. Then he swung another pass out to Levens for 13 yards. Finally the Pack had a first down at the Denver 31. That was when Brett and his team ran out of miracles.

Brett threw a bullet over the middle that Freeman couldn't hold. Then he tried to hit Robert Brooks for what would have been a first down, but safety Steve Atwater was there to break it up. And on fourth down, Brett threw over the middle for Mark Chmura, but linebacker John Mobley got a hand in and batted it away. That was it. Denver just had to run out the clock, and the AFC had its first victory in fourteen years. John Elway finally had his Super Bowl win.

The loss was a bitter disappointment for the Packers. Terrell Davis had been brilliant all afternoon. He ran for 157 yards on 30 carries and was named the game's Most Valuable Player. Elway was just 12 for 22 for 123 yards, but it was enough.

In the eyes of most, Brett was the better quarterback that afternoon, only he didn't quite live up to his Superman reputation. He completed 25 of 42 passes for 256 yards and 3 touchdowns. He had one pass picked off and fumbled once.

Though the loss was a bitter disappointment, Brett made no excuses. "We didn't have it today," he said. "I overthrew [Freeman] by a hair down the sideline and just missed the pass to Robert

Brooks on the last drive. Sometimes you make the plays, and sometimes you don't. We scored three touchdowns, and it should have been enough. It wasn't."

The game would be analyzed and dissected for weeks. Bronco defensive back Ray Crockett said Brett often won by taking risks, but it was the risks that got him in trouble in the Super Bowl. Others said the Packers lost because their defense wore down and allowed Terrell Davis to run wild. Others said the Packers had read too many of their own clippings and had come in overconfident.

The bottom line was that a second straight Super Bowl just wasn't to be. Green Bay would have to wait till next year, as so many other teams have done. The Denver Broncos were simply the better team on this particular day.

The loss certainly didn't diminish the respect everyone had for Brett Favre.

After the game, Brett bumped into Bronco safety Steve Atwater. The two embraced, and Atwater said what so many others were thinking. "You're a true champion," he said to Brett.

At the tender age of twenty-eight, Brett Favre has almost lived a lifetime. There have been battles both on and off the field, obstacles to overcome, a talent to develop. Yet he has triumphed to become one of the National Football League's most outstanding players, a tremendous quarterback, and a charismatic leader whom fans all around the league flock to see.

He became a starter for the Green Bay Packers at the age of twenty-two, and hasn't missed a game since. He has a wife, a daughter, and a loving family to support him. Despite all his trials and tribulations, he considers himself a very lucky guy. And for those reasons he has also begun to give back.

In 1995 Brett helped raise more than $80,000 for the Boys and Girls Club of Green Bay by donating $150 for each of his touchdown passes and for each of the team's rushing TDs. He also arranged for matching corporate contributions and has continued the practice ever since.

The Brett Favre Foundation, started in 1996, raises money for three youth-oriented charities—the Special Olympics, Cystic Fibrosis, and the Boys and Girls Clubs.

That isn't all. Brett also hosts the annual Brett Favre Celebrity Golf Outing, which generates additional revenues for his foundation. He is also involved with the annual Punt, Pass, and Kick competition held each year for youngsters all around the country.

But what most people want to see is Brett running the Green Bay offense, throwing his powerful passes downfield, exhorting his team to win, win, win. At age twenty-eight, he still has a long future before him, a lot of passes to throw, and many more games to win. The quarterback from the Deep South, who loves playing in the frozen North is, as Steve Atwater and so many other have said, "a true champion."

His philosophy is simple, and it never changes. He stated it very well in an interview during the 1997 season: "I'm never satisfied. I'm always frightened that someone will take my place. So whenever I go out on the field, I just want to be the very best."

About the Author

Bill Gutman has been a freelance writer for more than twenty years. In that time he has written over 150 books for children and adults, many of which are about sports. He has written profiles and biographies of many sports stars from both past and present, as well as writing about all the major sports, and some lesser ones as well. Aside from biographies, his sports books include histories, how-to instructionals, and sports fiction. He is the author of Archway's *Sports Illustrated* series; biographies of Bo Jackson, Michael Jordan, Shaquille O'Neal, Grant Hill, Tiger Woods, Ken Griffey, Jr., and Brett Favre; and *NBA High-Flyers*, profiles of top NBA stars. All are available from Archway Paperbacks. Mr. Gutman currently lives in Dover Plains, New York, with his wife and family.

KOBE BRYANT: A Biography

by Jonathan Hall

Get on the ball and find out the inside story of one of basketball's hottest, and youngest, stars—Kobe Bryant. From a childhood in Italy, to being the youngest player ever selected in the NBA draft, to being voted as the youngest starter ever for an NBA all-star game, Kobe amazes fans and players with his moves on and off the court. But how did this young man become so famous at such an early age? Pick up a copy of this action-packed biography to find out if he's the next Michael Jordan —or the first Kobe Bryant.

Available in mid-January 1999

From Archway Paperbacks
Published by Pocket Books

2009

Ken Griffey Jr.
A Biography

Follow the path of Ken Griffey Jr., from his days as a troubled teenage phenom to his current status as baseball's best all-around player. It's the inspirational story of one of sports' most popular heroes.

By
Bill Gutman

Available from Archway Paperbacks
Published by Pocket Books

1454-01